The Yuma Sanction

Escape from Yuma? They claimed it was impossible, but lifer Dev Vallery did it. But escaping from Arizona's hell-on-earth prison was one thing and staying free another, as he was to learn when the manhunter marshal camped on his trail.

Vallery should have been running scared. Instead he built a new life ramrodding cattle, only to realize that Braden, the boss, was more dangerous than any lawman could ever be.

Now Vallery must cut loose with blazing guns to challenge his fate and defy *The Yuma Sanction*.

The Yuma Sanction

MATT JAMES

A Black Horse Western

ROBERT HALE · LONDON

© Matt James 2005
First published in Great Britain 2005

ISBN 0 7090 7671 1

Robert Hale Limited
Clerkenwell House
Clerkenwell Green
London EC1R 0HT

Typeset by
Derek Doyle & Associates, Liverpool.
Printed and bound in Great Britain by
Antony Rowe Limited, Wiltshire

CHAPTER 1

HOBO TOWN BLUES

Vallery came into Muleshoe in the dark of the night. The moon was a feeble slice in the sky, the stars too few to shed light. He walked with the reins of his dusty horse looped over his left arm, right hand not far from his gun. The drunk contesting salvage rights over a can of trash with a gaunt-ribbed dog, turned and called something after him, but he kept walking, his face shadowed beneath his hat and the yellow glow of a rickety streetlight falling briefly across weary shoulders.

He walked slowly, scuffed boots dragging a little in the gravel. He felt the legacy of the long miles behind him most in his legs and the small of his back. Ground-lanterns and oil-lamps threw yellow, muted light into the shadows. He saw two saloons, a high-balconied hotel blotting out the feeble stars and, a half-block further west, a squat adobe building with bars on its windows and a faded sign that said simply: Sheriff.

5

He halted, tight white lines cutting the corners of his mouth. He'd hoped Muleshoe might prove too small to boast its own law office, but it was beginning to look bigger than it had at first appeared. For just a moment he considered grabbing a bite and moving on. Then he took a look at the horse, licked dry lips and headed on towards the smaller and rougher-looking of the two saloons on Sundown Street.

This man needed a drink and a feed, while the horse wouldn't be fit to ride until daybreak at the earliest. He would take his chances.

He saw a tall powerful-looking figure in an ankle-length duster mount the steps of the saloon of his choice and vanish inside. He tied up at the hitch rail and mounted the steps, heavy-footed and slow, and crossed to the grimed window. A man like him couldn't be too careful anyplace and that went double in a strange town.

The Dirty Shame appeared to be well-named, but squinting through the grimed glass the traveller geared up his optimism in the dim hope that he would sight – despite the squalor and liquored-up racket rocking the place – that he still might sight a ruddy-cheeked and animated mine host just waiting to welcome any bone-weary trailsman who happened by to come through his batwings with a raging thirst and silver dollars in his Levis.

Some hope.

There was nothing welcoming about swag-bellied Sam Pickett; his leather-lined features were as sallow and sour as a bucket of swill.

6

The only things animated about the boss of the Dirty Shame were his tiny pig eyes as they fastened on the big stranger in the grey duster who just a minute earlier had come slamming through his scarred old doors with a great rush and clatter before propping to stare about him as he fingered back his hat.

Trouble.

Bossing the bar of the roughest saloon in Muleshoe day in and day out as Pickett did, a man developed a sixth sense about people. You got so you could virtually guarantee which newcomer was merely going to stand across from you soaking up the hard stuff until he fell in a heap, and which one was going to raise some hell.

The broad-shouldered, square-jawed man in the tailored broadcloth travelling-suit and grey duster fitted so neatly into the latter category that he might have created it. He talked way too loud, dressed too well and was already flashing a big roll of notes as he ordered drinkers from his path and headed for the bar.

Pickett sighed. A man of this stranger's years and obvious prosperity should know how not to conduct himself in a strange town in a tough bar, he mused. Or could be he was simply drunk, although he sure didn't look it.

'Whiskey!' Rand Braden shouted, banging a fist down on the bartop. 'And I mean real whiskey, mister, not the slop you serve up to the losers and know-nothings!'

Pickett shook his head as he reached for his best

bottle. His saloon, which stood on Muleshoe's Sundown Street between a buffalo-hide storehouse and the burnt-out ruin of the old Star Hotel, was crowded this cold spring night. Its clients were the roughest types in town – buffalo-butchers, petty hustlers, sneak thieves, several troopers on leave from the fort, gamblers, drunks and big rough working men in denim and soiled leather jackets. Almost everyone looked either mean or dangerous – and right now they all seemed to be staring at the newcomer, who was slapping the bar and ordering the saloonman to get a shake on.

'Stranger,' Pickett said quietly, 'ain't you got no horse sense at all?'

'What?' Braden's whiskey-thickened voice was laced with arrogance and authority. He was a man accustomed to giving orders and having them obeyed without question. He could buy a dump like this with his small change.

The saloon boss leaned closer. 'Take a look around. Some of the geezers here ain't seen as much *dinero* as you're flashing around in all their goddamn lives, let alone in one lump. So do us both a favor and put it away, will you?'

'You're giving me advice?'

'Right.'

'Right. Now I'll give you some. Pass me that glass, make my change and keep your fool mouth shut or I'll shut it for you!'

Braden was a rich and powerful man with a natural steamrolling style, yet was rarely this offensive, particularly when alone and far from home. The truth of it was, he had outsized business problems which he'd hoped to solve here, but things hadn't panned out his way. A hundred miles from his sprawling cattle empire and without his customary protection, he should have been more discreet than to drink too much and throw his weight around, but discretion had never been part of his make-up. Sensing this, Pickett did as ordered then stepped back to watch the 'fun'.

It wasn't long in coming. Before the stranger was half-way through his drink the toughest joint in town began living up to its reputation. Like vultures, they began closing in from all sides. The whores reached him first, flaunting their wares and calling him 'big boy'. A disgruntled cowboy scented a natural enemy – a rich rancher – and a pard was holding him back from taking a swing at the newcomer, just for the hell of it. Pickpockets were trying to break through and footpads lurked by the batwings, like buzzards at a funeral. The rest just watched, curious and attentive.

As though oblivious to it all Braden threw his whiskey down his throat, bad-mouthed a whore and her sinister pimp, banged his glass on the bar for another. The roll made another appearance and a hulking bum yelled:

'Hey, that's my goddamn money. This bastard must have picked my pocket!'

Drinkers laughed.

'Don't let him scare you none, sweetie,' a woman with cheeks as red as blood reassured the cattleman. 'He's just tryin' it on. He ain't had two white dimes to rub together since he stopped rollin' drunks to take up panhandlin'.'

The raw-boned loser seized the hustler by the shoulder and sent her reeling. He loomed before Braden, his manner ugly and threatening now.

'I want my money, joker.'

Braden grinned. He seemed to be relishing the situation.

'You say this is your money, friend?'

'Sure 'nuff.'

'Then why don't you try to take it – scum?'

The big man blinked, taken aback by such aggression, wondering if he'd picked the wrong mark. The whore laughed scornfully. The big man's face flushed and he lunged forward. A lightning punch smashed his nose. Moving in fast before he could recover, Braden kneed to the groin then rabbit-punched to the neck. The troublemaker's face was ashen as he thudded to his knees, blowing spittle from his mouth.

Grinning, enjoying himself, Braden stepped back a pace, measured the man off then kicked him in the belly.

An angry rumble rose from the mob as the bloody-faced hustler rolled on to his back, gasping for breath. Before anybody could intervene, the stranger kicked to the ribs and then to the head with a big flash boot fashioned from Spanish leather.

It took a lot to impress the clients of Pickett's bar but that did the trick. A minute previously they'd assessed the stranger as that rarest of all bonanzas – a boozing, well-heeled fool all alone, acting up and just begging to be taken. Suddenly they were aware that he didn't appear quite as drunk as he was acting and might even appear pretty dangerous as he backed up to the bar with one hand resting on gunbutt.

They were wise to be cautious. Where the big man hailed from, he had men with guns to watch his back. But it hadn't always been that way. On his way up the ladder, Rand Braden had done all his own rough-housing and shot his own meat and cooked it.

'Anyone else with a claim on my roll?'

No takers.

'Just like I figured.' Contemptuously now, Braden let go of the gun, tugged at his duster and deliberately turned his back. He slapped the bartop. 'Two fingers, barslop, and make it snappy!'

Pickett was quick to oblige and Braden drank off half the whiskey at a gulp before returning his attention to the quiet room. His lip curled in a sneer.

'You know, this beats all. Here I am, a man with more money than sense . . . obviously. At least that's obvious to me now. When I set out to travel eighty miles just to check out a town with a tough reputation in search of something I've been looking for for three lousy weeks on the road, I thought I was being real smart. "You want tough men, you'll find them in spades in Muleshoe." That's what I was told. But I saw the moment I walked in here that walking eighty inches – never mind miles – would have been way too far just to look over the trash I'm looking at right now.'

They had no notion what he was talking about. But they were curious. The unlikely combination of a fat roll, big mouth and an impressive talent for rough-housing all wrapped up in one outsized stranger was something this hardcase town hadn't encountered before.

'What you've been looking for?' prompted Pickett, as curious as any. 'And what might that be, sir?'

'Talent, of course.'

'What kind of talent?' someone wanted to know.

For a long moment it appeared the man couldn't be bothered answering. Then he sighed and seemed to lose some of his aggressive energy.

'What kind?' he echoed. 'What other kind is there? Ranch talent, of course. You're looking at a man with forty thousand acres of prime grazeland and more cattle than he can count who's just spent three weeks he can ill afford searching for a man or the men with the guts and knowhow to help him run a big spread so that one man – me – isn't forced to carry the whole damned weight on his own shoulders.'

'You're looking for ranch hands?' Pickett asked. 'That all?'

'All?' the cattleman snapped back. 'Mister, I've checked out maybe thirty–forty likely men in the past three weeks and came up with nothing but gutless wonders, know-nothings and deadbeats.'

His gesture encompassed the saloon.

'This was my last long shot, so that should give you some idea how desperate I've been getting. Bumtown USA!' He sneered. 'I wouldn't hire any

man in this burg to swamp out my latrines on the
Buffalo Gate . . . and that goes for you too, barkeep –
whatever your name is. So pour me another so I can
drown my sorrows, then I'll be on my way home
before whatever it is about this town that turns men
into trash on two legs gets me too. C'mon, c'mon,
don't just stand there looking stupid!'

He was overdoing it again, stoking the furnaces. It
was likely true that any man searching for range
talent would be hard put to find a less promising
town than Muleshoe. But there was talent aplenty
beneath these smoking hanging lights – talent asso-
ciated with a sap to the back of the head, a knee to
the groin and skill with a Bowie knife or garrotte if
and when things got really out of hand.

Braden might have seen this had he been less
affected by weariness and disappointment. Might
have seen that Muleshoe wasn't short of genuine
hard men; and even bums have their pride . . .

'The hell!' he snorted abruptly. He swung from
the bar and headed for the batwings in the same
headlong way he'd entered.

Nobody tried to halt him and maybe eagle-eyed
Pickett was the only one to notice a trio of his most
dangerous customers quietly finish their drinks and
leave soon after, ambling outside like men with nothing to do and all night to do it in.

By this, the liquored-up stranger was half-way
along the block, leaning against an upright as he
waited for the street to stop heaving in his vision.
This took some time, but eventually he was able to
straighten. He fingered back his beaver hat.

You've drunk too much, Braden, he told himself with a self-indulgent grin. Again. He laughed and slammed a fist into the post. Or maybe not. Wonder if a man could find a place that sells even worse booze than that flea-trap?

He started off with his long assured stride, duster flapping in the wind. The street he followed off main was no place for rich strangers to explore late at night, but even had he known it that wouldn't have stopped him.

Hobo Town was the slum quarter of Muleshoe and South Street cut clear through its seedy heart.

A beggar leaned from a shadowy doorway.

'Alms for the poor, mister?'

'Cut a vein.'

The man hobbled after him, looking like just another South Street derelict. But he wasn't. Cutter Bilk had witnessed the recent scene at the Dirty Shame and quit the dive with his henchmen right after the cattleman left. Cutter was offended, greedy and highly dangerous. His partners watched from cover across the street as he stumbled convincingly after his mark.

'Just a few lousy cents, mister,' he called plaintively. 'I ain't ate all day long.'

There was eagerness in Braden's face as he whirled with fists cocked. Tomorrow it would be reality, a hangover and a certain sense of failure – but he wasn't through having his fun tonight.

He threw a haymaker. Cutter appeared to stumble. He lurched against Braden, who brushed him roughly aside. The moment he felt his sixshooter leave its holster, the warning bell clanged in in the cattleman's skull. He grabbed a ragged arm and swung a blow that missed by fully a foot, as dark shapes rushed from their cover behind.

'Take him, boys!' Cutter hissed, and lashed out savagely with his own revolver.

The blow grazed Braden's brow as he ducked. He broke clear and began to run, sobering fast and fully realizing his danger in a moment. Bragging and brawling under bright saloon lights was a far cry from tangling with a knifer gang in a fetid alley.

The shadowy derelicts and cackling crones of Hobo Town watched excitedly from leaning hovels as a well-dressed man pounded by with Cutter Bilk and his boys in close pursuit. If the sheriff were to find a cut-up corpse in the morning, none of these night people would have seen a blessed thing.

At full stretch now, Braden slewed around a foggy corner and pounded on down a long unlit side lane. Something hissed past his ear and he heard the knife clatter against the stones a short distance ahead. He pumped his knees and glanced over his shoulder to see that they were keeping pace, gaining maybe.

It was like running through a foggy tunnel with the echoes of their flying feet bouncing back from fetid walls. Braden cursed the thieves, the darkness and his own foolhardiness. Never again! he promised as he hurtled by a ruined brick wall, leapt a discarded plank and rushed on. If he survived this he would embrace the prudence and self-control that had always eluded him. If . . .

Another alley. Long and twisting, with lines of washing hanging overhead. He charged headlong down it. The steps seemed to be drawing closer behind. He plunged across an intersecting laneway, saw lights somewhere ahead, maybe a million miles away. A knife glanced off his back with a quick flick of pain before clattering loose. He looked back to see he was now actually making headway. He felt a surge of hope rise for a split second, then he slammed into something solid and went down. On hands and knees he shook his head, dimly aware he'd run straight into a fence in the darkness. A triumphant cry from behind saw him struggle to one knee. He fumbled to grasp at a broken paling but knew he would never get to use it as the three menacing shapes loomed above him.

'Come on you bastards!' he shouted defiantly. 'One at a time or all at once. It's all the same to me!'

They came in a rush.

Dev Vallery looked up from his glass.

'You say something?' he said.

'Huh?'

'Just asked if you heard something.'

'Like what?'

'Like . . . well, like someone runnin' by like they was in a big hurry, I guess.'

Vallery surveyed the tiny room. It was called a saloon but was no more than a clapboard cubby nailed on to a blacksmith's shed, furnished by a plank bar supported by two kegs and three sets of rickety tables and chairs. He was the only customer,

16

the big-nosed bartender the only staff.

'Maybe I did,' he grunted. 'But that wouldn't be unusual down here, would it? Folks running, I mean.'

'Down here' comprised a squalid dead-end lane running off a wide and muddy street that led straight for the river. It was the sort of place that made the Dirty Shame look plush. But Joe's suited this man far better. The lights had been too bright at the Shame, the prices too high. In addition, this dive boasted no bigmouth flashing his money about under the noses of a crowd that had looked like they'd rob their own mothers.

He'd taken all that in at a glance uptown and simply headed into Hobo Town where Bob's single smoking lantern and wide open spaces drew him like a magnet.

'Guess it ain't so unusual at that,' Bob conceded at last. 'Runnin' folks, I mean. Down here.'

Vallery shrugged, ready to let it go. He had heard strange noises moments earlier, could still hear them faintly but chose to ignore them. If there was real trouble abroad on this town's seedy side tonight he didn't want to know about it. He had his reasons.

Then: 'Yonder goes that sonuva, Cutter! Headin' across the lot like a huntin' dog!'

The shout coming through the single window was swallowed by another distant shout followed by a curse. The two men's eyes met, Dev's questioning, the saloonman's filled with genuine alarm.

'They call him Cutter on account he cuts folks, mister . . .'

17

Vallery cursed under his breath, tossed change on the table and ducked through the hessian-hung doorway. Habits of a lifetime are hard to break. Sounded like someone might be in real trouble out there.

It took seconds to adjust his vision to the thick gloom. He glimpsed movement beyond the unlighted intersection where a gaunt dead tree leaned at a drunken angle over a vacant lot.

As he stared, a dim figure lunged into view on the far side of the lot and clambered over a pile of broken packing crates before vanishing again.

There was no identifying the man at this distance. But how many Hobo Towners sported ankle-length grey dusters?

He cursed softly.

He knew it had to be the same big-mouth he'd sighted throwing his weight and his money around at the Dirty Shame; the trouble-hunter who'd prompted him to head for Joe's.

Why the hell wasn't he surprised?

He stiffened as something flashed momentarily over there; like light on steel, maybe.

He swore as he broke into a long-legged lope and headed for the intersection. He crossed over and followed the sounds of running feet as they led him through an untidy scatter of tin-roofed shanties, around the splintered ruins of a cow corral, then on into the jaws of a wide-mouthed alley which seemed as dark as the inside of a cow until he caught the glimpse of a pale face over yonder by a dangerously tilted wall, realized immediately that there were more faces and shapes, in those shadows – a mêlée.

And the biggest figure in the bunch wore a grey dust-coat and cursed like a muleskinner!

For just one hanging moment, Dev Vallery's integrity struggled with his survival instincts. Then he went forward, with his long-barrelled Peacemaker .45 hissing from its holster as he ran.

Now he saw blades glittering dully, and damned if the duster wasn't still cussing and throwing wild haymakers like he was either too drunk or too dumb to realize what deadly trouble he was in.

A high-backed figure loomed before him. He swung the gun hard, smashed the back of the knifer's head and dropped him flat without even a yell.

Instantly a runt with a Bowie and a feral with baleful yellow glare whirled to face the sudden danger.

But they were too slow and unsure compared with a rugged man of the outdoors, seasoned and rendered dangerous by circumstances not of his own making.

Vallery's swinging gun broke an ugly face open in a spray of crimson, and as he fell the third man uttered a sharp cluck of alarm and took off into the darkness.

Suddenly Dev was alone with a muddied figure in a tattered grey duster who gusted his boozy breath all over him and seemed to be attempting to hug him. Vallery shoved the gun in his face.

'Sober up, damn you!' he snarled, aware of lights going on, voices in the night. 'I'm getting the hell out of here and you can come if you want, I don't give a damn! I'm gone!'

He was as good as his word. Leaping a trash pile he immediately broke into a run.

'Hey, sonny, goddamnit, hold up. I wanna make you rich.'

Vallery kept running.

CHAPTER 2

THE CONTRACT

They eventually came to a grey frame-building on a rickety side street, which bore the single faded word LIVERY above the double doors. It was decrepit, like everything in Muleshoe, with cobwebs dangling from the eaves and the faint smell of decay.

Dev Vallery indicated the shadowy building in back of the stables.

'Ma Hendry's rooming-house. That's where I'm staying. If you want you can check in there later. I don't expect those bums to come looking for us, but in case they do we'll kill a little time in here.' He swung the door open. 'Feel like a drink?'

Puzzlement clouded the rancher's face. Braden was a hard man to faze but had been truly shaken up by what had very plainly been a dangerous situation. And for one of the rare times of his life, he was genuinely grateful; grateful and intrigued. Back in Hobo Town this tall, big-shouldered stranger with

21

the trimmed van Dyke beard and mustache had impressed powerfully both in the way he'd come to his aid and particularly in the masterful way he'd dealt with the footpads.

Yet with the danger plainly behind them, the man who'd introduced himself simply as 'Dev', now appeared quiet and watchful.

Not that Rand Braden really gave a damn about that. What signified was that this man had saved his life and he wanted to let him know how grateful he was.

As soon they were seated inside the stables with a turned-down lantern shedding a soft glow, Dev silently proffered a flask of rum as the cattleman produced the billfold the knifers had craved so badly.

'I'm a shaken-up man, son, and I hope I'm a man who's learned a big lesson tonight. But one kind of man I'm not, is a tightwad.'

He held up the roll he'd been flashing around at the Dirty Shame and began peeling off big-denomination notes.

'What Braden owes Braden pays, and he owes you big time.'

Vallery looked offended.

'Put your money away, mister. I'd have done what I did for anybody.'

'But the important thing is you did it for Rand Braden.' The rancher flashed his big dangerous smile. 'Wager you've heard of me, huh? Buffalo Gate Ranch? Biggest cow outfit in Waterquick County?'

'Sorry.'

'Well, I know you've heard of being poor. Can't

help noticing you look kind of the lean and hungry type, mister. C'mon, here's five hundred.'

'Put it away, damnit!'

The cattleman stared, studying his Samaritan for the first time by lantern light. He was looking at a handsome, grey-eyed man of around thirty with a rangy build, a strong jaw, neat beard and, yes – he was sure of it now – the strapping look of a man of the land.

'Whatever you say,' he said easily, neatly folding the money back into his billfold and slipping it into an inside pocket. He took a swig of the bottle and passed it across, his interest deepening by the moment. 'I don't want to be nosy, Dev, but what were you doing down there in the slums?'

'Minding my own business, I guess.'

Braden spread his hands wide; he could be charming when it suited.

'Look, believe me, I'm not being nosy. But when a total stranger risks his life for a man . . . But the heck with that if you don't want to talk about it. Can I ask you something else? You're a cowman, aren't you?'

'Was once.'

'Working now?' Braden's mind was jumping ahead. Vallery shook his head, and Braden leaned forward. 'Would you believe I'm looking for a top hand – or hands – right now. Matter of fact I just gave myself three weeks' leave to find what I need right at the start of the busy season.' He gestured. 'But I've found out that looking for something you want and getting it can be two mighty different things. Man, the bums and losers and hopefuls I've seen, you just wouldn't believe. Although if you were to take a quick look about this dump – the last on my list, by the way – you'd know what I mean. Then suddenly, through pure luck, I'm staring at what I've been looking for.'

'Not interested.'

'But you don't know what I'm offering . . .'

Braden broke off at a sound. It was only a horse shifting in its stall, yet Vallery rose quickly and went to the doors to peer out. But not so quickly that the sharp-eyed cattleman didn't notice how, as he'd reached up for a crossbeam to haul himself off his low stool, his jacket cuff had ridden up his arm some to reveal a scar on the wrist that caused his eyes to stretch wide and set his scheming mind into over-drive.

Dev returned and took a swab of cotton waste from a water bucket to dab at the mouse under his eye. His left cheekbone had been deeply grazed in the brawl but he seemed indifferent to any discomfort.

While the seated cattle-king was thinking: cattle-man, horseman, strong character, fighter, hard as nails, high principles and, most important of all – American! The whole goddamn package, just like I'd ordered him from a Sears Roebuck catalogue . . .'

Standing tall with the lamplight splashing up over his clean-cut features, Vallery caught that look and cocked an eyebrow.

'What?' he he demanded suspiciously.

'Nothing,' Braden insisted. Yet he couldn't conceal his excitement as he suddenly jumped erect and spread both arms wide, a characteristic gesture.

'Ahh, hell and goddamnit, let's cut the buffalo dust, *amigo*. Get down to cases, I mean. I need a top hand and you need work and money.' He shrugged. 'You saved my life and I want to repay you. Anything strange about that? Come work for me for top dollar at the work you know best.'

'No.'

'What do you mean – no? You can't afford to—'

'I can afford anything I like. Look, Braden, I know you appreciate what I did. But let's let it lie at that. I'm riding out at first light and that's how I like it. If I wanted work I'd take your offer, but I don't.'

'Better than working on a chain-gang, mister.'

Vallery's hand dropped to gunbutt, grey eyes suddenly dangerous. 'Just what the hell do you mean by that?'

Braden folded his arms and looked more confident by the moment, more certain of where his suspicions were taking him now.

'It all fits. A big strong feller with class stamped all over him riding around on his lonesome on a broken-down horse without two white dimes in his Levis. Comes to a nothing town but dodges the bright lights and the saloons to hole up on the wrong side of the tracks. Works over a bunch of toughs like a pro, turns down big money and a big chance for no good reason, just wants to get moving again. What does all that add up to to you, Dev?'

'You tell me, wiseacre.'

'All that . . . plus that scar on your wrist?' Braden grinned broadly. 'You're on the dodge, cowboy.'

'You're loco!'

'We both know that just ain't so.'

Vallery took out the makings and began fashioning a cigarette. A late-night horseman went clip-clopping by along the road. He finished twisting his smoke into shape and set it alight with steady fingers. Over the tiny flame, his eyes drilling at Braden were chips of ice.

'You'd better leave, mister,' he said quietly. 'That flapping mouth of yours could give you more trouble than you know.'

For the first time in a hectic night which had seen his nerve tested to the limit, Braden showed a flicker of unease. So he grinned, another habit.

'Damnit, you're right, Dev. Seems I'm always bolting ahead of myself and getting into trouble as a consequence. Look, maybe if I told you a little more about myself you'd realize I'm straight as a gunbarrel and mean you no harm, only a whole heap of good.'

'I doubt it.'

'Let me paint the picture plain. Back on Buffalo Gate, I'm king. I boss more land than I can cover in a week's riding and more Mex cowhands than you could count. Day to day I have to deal with rustlers, loafing hands, tightwad bankers and people who plain hate my guts just because I'm Braden and they are nothing. You wouldn't know what it's like to stand that tall, but I can tell you it gets hard to take. There's no way a man like me can relax and let his hair down, not even for a day, which is half the reason I've been acting so foolish and headstrong tonight. Letting off steam. I've got to head home tomorrow, without the men I wanted, and when I get back there I'll be back in that prison of my own making again. That's why I'm jumping ahead like a bull at a gate with you. I'm desperate. I mightn't look it but that is the goddamned truth. Do you believe me?'

Maybe he did and maybe not. But Vallery's annoyance was fading while his perceptive eye was working overtime. He'd been aware of the enormous power in that big body during the ruckus, didn't doubt the man was every bit as important as he claimed. He didn't like Rand Braden any more than he'd done from the outset, yet he impressed as a man.

But not a man he felt he could trust, certainly not somebody he would be prepared to work for.

Sure, he knew he could handle the job he'd been offered; he knew more about cows than he did about pretty women. But Dev Vallery couldn't afford to take a job any time, any place. He was condemned to keep riding with a gun always at the ready and a suspicious eye for anyone who crossed his path. He went to the door and peered out.

'Street's quiet now. I'll walk you back to the hotel, just in case there's any trouble still about.'

For just a moment, staring at the other's lean back, Braden's dark eyes flared like an animal's. But as Dev turned, big teeth flashed and he shrugged.

'Well, a man can only try, I guess. We'd have made a good team but it wasn't to be. Don't let it be said Rand Braden can't take a disappointment. Lead on, Macduff.'

The three-block walk to the hotel proved uneventful and Vallery left Braden smiling from the door and waving, just like they were old friends parting. He was almost out on his feet by the time he got back to his quarters, where he stretched out on his bunk without even bothering to remove his boots.

He didn't dream.

He awoke just before dawn as he'd done every day of his life on his four-section spread clear across the territory. There was no sign of Ma Hendry when he went through to the kitchen after shaving in the bathroom, so he lit the stove and fixed himself some eggs, his movements unhurried and efficient. He studied his face in a spoon and saw that the bruising hadn't come to much.

His tongue poked at a sore tooth. In retrospect it had been a tolerably dangerous brawl. He was sure of one thing: Braden would have been done in if he hadn't got to him in time.

He half-smiled as he washed the dishes and put some money under the coffee-pot. You'd think he had enough troubles of his own without buying in on other people's. Maybe that was why he was a fugitive on the run and Braden was heading home south to a spread that sounded the size of a border province.

Warbag over his shoulder, Dev Vallery quit the rooming-house and walked across the yard towards the creaking old livery stable.

Moving on . . .

How many times in the past months had he quit a place silently in the small hours, heading on to he knew not where? He'd lost count of the lonesome high-country camps, the seedy rooming-houses, the back streets where a running man could hide. . . .

It hadn't always been that way. Until a few months back he'd never known what it was like to hide from anybody, fear anything, be accountable to no man. Hadn't previously experienced the sensation of jolting awake in the middle of the night, his heart pounding, wondering if that faint noise that had awakened him was just the wind or the stealthy step of a man with a badge and a gun. Until then it had been all pride and achievement; now all was lost . . . gone with the bullet that had snuffed out a rich man's life. . . .

His horse whickered as he entered the livery. Vallery set his warbag aside and hauled his saddle off the tree. He'd planned on resting up a few days in Muleshoe, but that wouldn't be safe now. As he cinched up the leathers he knew he couldn't afford to take risks, even if his horse was beat and himself not that much flasher. He'd bought into a brawl and that sort of thing got around, maybe reach as far as uptown where the lawman hung his hat.

Lawmen, like good times, peaceful nights, friendships and public places were just a few of the things a man gave up on when he took to the owlhoot trail.

The saddling completed, he looped the bridle over his arm, turned for the doorway, and froze.

Rand Braden completely filled the doorway with his wide-shouldered six feet four.

'Early start, eh, Dev?' The man's eyes were sly. 'Well, I guess I can understand that.'

Vallery's jaw muscles worked.

'What the hell do you want, Braden?'

'Does a man have to want something just on account he—'

29

'Cut the crap.'

Vallery's bronzed hand rested on gunbutt. This man's being here didn't hit him right, and that smirk wasn't making him feel any more relaxed.

'OK, OK, Dev, no call to get all hostile.'

Braden was toting a rolled-up document of some kind. Without speaking, he snapped it open. In the dim light, Vallery stared at the crude black-and-white woodcut illustration of his own face without the beard and mustache he'd cultivated to disguise it. Beneath the picture in heavy black type were the words:

Wanted for Murder
Devereaux Vallery
Reward $1000

There was a congealing silence. For a moment Vallery didn't seem to breathe as his eyes lifted from the wanted dodger to the smirking face above it. He was listening intently for a sound, any sound that might suggest that men with badges and guns might be lurking on the other side of the stable walls.

'Struck dumb, eh, Dev?' Braden laughed softly. 'Struck dumb, Dev? Well, I can understand that, I guess—'

He got no further. Two lunging strides carried Vallery to his man. The blow he threw had so much rage and power behind it that Braden was driven six feet to crash into a wall, bringing down an empty grain-bin with a great clatter as he slumped unconscious to the straw.

Vallery didn't see him fall. He lunged through the doorway with a cocked Colt in his fist, fully expecting to find the stables surrounded by men with guns.

Not a soul in sight.

He dashed to the corner of the building and faced the street. It was as empty as a rooming-house pantry. Slowly he lowered his weapon and absently sucked skinned knuckles. He remembered Braden. He hurried back inside and found that the big man had actually made it back to his hands and knees. He must have a granite jaw.

He hooked a hand under his armpit and heaved him erect. Braden spat blood and wiggled a tooth with his fingers. When he looked at Vallery his eyes were crossed. He banged his temple with the heel of his hand and his eyeballs clicked back into symmetry as though his head was a slot machine.

'I . . . I should be mad, Dev . . . but I'm not. When I think on how handy a right hook like that's going to be on Buffalo Gate, why, I just feel excited.'

'Shut up. How did you come by that poster?'

'Law office, of course. They've got sheaves of them up there.'

'What made you go looking for it there, you swivel-eyed son of a bitch?'

The big man sobered.

'I told you you had owlhoot written all over you, son. Tried my level best to get you to play my way, but when you acted cute and wouldn't 'fess up, why, I just had to go looking for proof.'

'I could kill you right where you stand!'

'Wouldn't that be foolish, man? Sheriff Brown is a tough old rooster. He'd chase you and catch you, then they'd have to hang you twice. Once for me and once for this other gent you put in the ground. Brewster, they call him in the fine print. What'd you murder him for, son?'

Suddenly all Vallery's strength seemed to leave him at once. Like an old man he moved inside the stables and sat on a bench. He stared down at his hands, waiting for the trembling to leave his limbs as the nightmare whirled through his brain ... the killing of the rich Mexican rancher, visiting Flint River on business ... his false arrest ... trial ... conviction ... chain-gang weeks while they prepared to ship him to Yuma to begin a life stretch ... a guard's momentary carelessness leading to his desperate escape ... the fugitive trail ever since. ...

He grew aware of two legs standing before him. He looked up.

'If you didn't turn me in then get the hell out of my life before I kill you, Braden.'

'Sorry.'

'What the hell do you mean by that?'

Braden explained.

He was sorry for Vallery's situation, he insisted, but characteristically was infinitely more sympathetic to Rand Braden. His largely unexplained situation back at home was still bordering on the critical, or so he claimed; he was still desperately in need of a competent, reliable, American man of the land as a 'kind of ramrod'.

Said he'd really like to let Vallery just fork his bronc and wander off to the next Muleshoe or something worse, he really would.

But he couldn't.

He was out of time, had found the man he wanted, couldn't afford to leave go. He 'regretted' that; if Vallery turned him down again he'd feel obliged to alert the sheriff to the presence of a convicted killer in his town.

So, what did he say?

The man had guts, Dev conceded. For had he been a real killer he might well have drawn his pistol then and there and used it.

Then again, Braden was a smart *hombre*, he mused. The man had probably read him like a book and likely realized he was no killer.

He shook his head. The hell with figuring. It was really a simple decision to make. He could run and risk half the county chasing him half-way across the south-west on a played-out horse. Or else he could take up the offer to ramrod a cow empire in the South a good distance from the nearest town where a man might not see a John Law from one year's end to another.

He was too tired, beat and drained out right then even to figure out how he might free himself without risking losing everything.

Maybe Buffalo Gate Ranch was the only choice to make, so he made it.

'You won't regret it, Dev,' the rancher insisted, beaming widely despite one closed eye, a swollen lip and a rapidly bruising jaw.

Braden was wrong about that, Dev thought bitterly. He was already regretting it. But that didn't mean he wouldn't go through with it. He'd given his word, and self-respect was one of the few things he had left.

CHAPTER 3

BUFFALO GATE

The way to Buffalo Gate took them through a land of high, flat mesas and little round hills spotted thinly with cedar bushes. The winter rains had brought generous grass coverage to the cattle lands, thick, substantial buffalo in low areas and a thin nourishing growth of gramma to the hills and high slopes.

It was springtime and gentle sunshine streamed warm and golden across the big land.

For the first fifty miles from Muleshoe their trail ran roughly parallel to the course of the meandering Chisos River. Then it branched sharply away, angling south-west, leaving the wide and shallow Chisos to snake away into the mesquite country and El Hondo.

Riding a pure-blood Arab stallion as befitted a man of his means, Rand Braden proved amiable enough during the first day's journey, but during the second Vallery noticed a change come over the man. The Braden he'd encountered in Muleshoe had

35

been a man in desperate search of relief from his heavy responsibilities wherever he might find it. He'd seemed pleased to sign him on. Yet the closer they drew to Waterquick County the more reserved and withdrawn he appeared to become. At times they would travel miles without a word passing between them, no sound other than the creak of saddle leather and the dull thud of hoofbeats in dust punctuated by the occasional call of a crow or bluejay.

Mile by mile, Rand Braden was resuming his Buffalo Gate face.

This bothered Vallery not at all – he welcomed it. Somehow he felt safe from pursuit and the reaching tentacles of the law down here and in this man's company, and found himself able to enjoy the ride. He relished the feeling of spring sun, the easy pace. Ever since breaking out of Flint River jail he'd mostly travelled by night and along the back trails, one hand on his gun and one eye on the trail in back of him. He hadn't been this deep south-west before and found the country unexpectedly lush and serene in contrast with where he'd lived before coming to grief.

Flint River.

Even the name sounded strange now, as if he'd left it years ago. He'd been respected there and had been on easy terms with the local sheriff, a situation that survived through his arrest and trial, but which came apart the night US Marshal Nells came to escort him to far Yuma to begin his life stretch.

In his mind's eye he saw the lawman go down under his manacled fists as he made his headlong charge for freedom. He'd found out later the lawman had not been seriously hurt. A good man, Nells, and a stubborn one. The fugitive knew it would be a long cold day in hell before US Marshal Nells closed the files on Dev Vallery.

They crossed the Buffalo Gate's eastern border just after four in the afternoon. They had ridden eighty miles from Muleshoe, a world away now, it seemed. It was a further ten miles to the ranch house and every inch of it belonged to the big man riding at his side.

As they crossed a low hill, Vallery spotted dust rising from brush country beyond the tree-line. Some distance further on they encountered a small herd being driven out of the timbered foothills to join a large gather lower down.

There were three cowhands in the party, all dressed in flapping leather chaps and the sombreros of *vaqueros*. The men halted and saluted on sighting them but Braden rode on unresponding, jaws clamped tightly, no sign of that big boozy grin from Muleshoe now.

The Mexicans turned stony-faced and sat their saddles in silence to watch them pass.

'I'm no hero here, Vallery,' he offered a short distance further along.

'Uh-huh.' Vallery was noncommittal. He planned to stay that way until he got a feel of this place, its people.

'Know what I am here?'

'What?'

Braden grimaced. 'The interloper, that's who. The

intruder, invader – the grab-all gringo. That's what I am. Me, an American on American soil. Can you believe it?' His sweeping gesture encompassed the cattle-graze stretching into hazy distances, seemingly to infinity.

'Before the pioneers spread south and west all this belonged to the Mexicans. It would likely still be theirs if they weren't so lazy, arrogant and proud and so convinced the old ways could never really change. In case you are wondering, I bought this land at a fair price, didn't just come in and grab it like so many others did.'

His mouth turned down at the corners.

'Though I doubt that I could be any less popular with the Mexes had I stolen the place from their don. They hate my guts.'

'And you hate theirs?'

'Every man Jack of them. They are scum.'

That seemed to take care of that.

They pushed on and eventually sighted another bunch of workers at a dipping-sluice.

'They seem to work pretty well whether they resent you or not, Braden.'

'Mister.'

'What?'

'I'm Mr Braden here. To everybody.'

'I don't call any man mister.'

'You'll get used to it.' Braden nodded in the direction of the sluices. 'But, yes, I suppose they are good workers. They know better than to be otherwise.' Braden took a long black cigar from a chased silver case and set it alight, eyes moving restlessly over his lands. He appeared to sit more ramrod-erect in the saddle and there was a more severe cut to his hard features. Coming on a man like this with no prior knowledge of him, Vallery mused, you would know intuitively he was someone riding his own acres, secure in his power and authority.

'These people work for me yet still dream of winning this land back.'

'Understandable, I guess. Seeing as it was theirs once.'

Braden glanced at him sharply. 'Nobody owns anything unless he's strong enough to hold it. You should know that. You had freedom and a good name once and couldn't hold on to either one.'

'At least I ain't scared.'

Braden flushed. 'Scared? You're accusing me of that? What do you mean?'

'You're scared they're going to win,' Vallery said with some satisfaction. 'That's why you're bragging it up to me. And that's why you hired me. Because you see me as tough enough – and American.' He held up a hand as the other made to retort. 'Relax. You can rely on me. You could have turned me in, so I owe you.'

A flicker of admiration crossed the big man's features.

'You're smart as well as capable, Vallery. I smelled that in you back at Muleshoe.' His gaze drifted. 'But you'll earn your money, mister. I've been shot at from ambush twice in the past six months.'

Dev nodded. Braden had correctly assessed his qualifications as a rancher, but it had been his other abilities which really interested him.

'You will be employed as a general ranch hand at first, mister, but your actual duties will extend far beyond that. I mightn't look it but in a way I'm a man under siege here. You see, I already have a body-guard, an impressive one as I know you will be forced to agree when you meet him. But Yancey, although powerful and dedicated, is slow and dull-witted. Fortunately I saw enough of you in Muleshoe to know you are neither. So, your main task will be to keep an ear to the ground, watch everybody closely and report back to me on anything that I might inter-pret as going against my interests. Is that clear?'

'Sounds like a big job.'

'You're being well paid.'

'Do you have any notion who tried to beef you?'

'Of course.' The big man shifted his weight in the saddle. 'If it wasn't my ramrod then he surely was the instigator.'

Vallery showed his surprise. The other smiled grimly.

'Yes, you're wondering: if I know who it was, why haven't I done something about him. But knowing and proving are two different things. Certainly, Miguel Sanchez is very different from the others – proud, dangerous, a born leader. As such, he's the only man who can keep the other Mexicans in line, so therefore he is indispensable. They regard him as their hero and would walk through fire for him.'

Vallery frowned. 'But if this is the case, why don't you fire him and the hands and hire an American crew?'

'Two factors. One, the *vaqueros* know every beast and every blade of grass on this place. They should. Mexicans owned it before me. The second reason is economics. I pay them fifteen dollars a month and found. An American, who wouldn't be half as useful, wouldn't work for double that. Beginning to make sense now?'

'Fifteen bucks a month. That's next door to starvation wages.'

'It's a tough world, Dev.'

Vallery fell silent and they rode on in silence. Passing through a grove of cottonwoods they emerged on a long grassy slope, and Vallery's keen eye was instantly caught by movement off to their left.

He reined in when he saw the tiny calf in the deep grass.

It was only a couple of days old, unsteady on spindly legs, obviously strayed from its mother. It was trying its legs out, running clumsily in short circles. Dev glanced at Braden who'd reined in a short distance ahead.

'Will we take him in?'

'The hands will spot it on their way home.'

Vallery grunted and was about to move his mount forward again when he spotted the eagle. It had already begun its swoop on the calf, dropping big and dark brown from the sky, wings swept back and lifted high and talons reaching for the strike.

He whipped his rifle from the scabbard, but the predator was rocketing in too swiftly for him. The eagle struck the calf and Vallery heard bone snap, sharp as the crack of a dry twig. Then the animal was down in the grass, kicking feebly with the bird crouched atop it.

In one fluent motion he threw the rifle to his shoulder and fired. The eagle shrieked in rage and lifted heavily into the air, shedding feathers. He fired again, the rifle jolting against his shoulder. The eagle burst apart in mid-air, wings flapping erratically as it fell. Vallery set his sights on the crippled calf and fired again. The tiny animal kicked and went still. He could feel Braden's stare upon him as he jacked the spent shell from the chamber and replaced it with another from his belt.

'Where did you learn to shoot like that?'

'Riding gun-guard on a stage line before I bought my own place. Why?'

'No reason,' came the reply. But the big man's expression seemed heavy with all kinds of considerations; he might have been impressed, wary, even uneasy at such a display; there was no telling which. 'Come on, we want to reach the house before dark.'

The remainder of the journey proved uneventful, until they raised the headquarters.

Dev had expected something impressive, but the reality was a shock. A splendid brick-and-adobe building, it stood on the side of a gentle slope surrounded by walled courts, painted outbuildings, corrals, orchards and breaking-yards, the plaster walls glowing a soft pink by the light of the dying sun.

He had seen great haciendas such as this along the valley from Taos to El Paso. With their wide lands about them, with their great storerooms filled with meat and grain, their troops of servants and their prolific women, they seemed as safe and permanent as anything man could build.

But up North the American invasion had all but wiped them out. The Mexicans were no good at business and and could no longer afford their mansions' massive upkeep in the face of gringo competition.

But there was no hint of decay here at the headquarters of Buffalo Gate Ranch – and for a moment Dev Vallery, ex-rancher and ex-free man was gripped by what almost amounted to a rage of envy.

Here was a man maybe just a few years his senior with everything a man could hope to possess, while he was a nothing – a loser with the law hunting him – no land, no home, not even a woman to call his own.

'Something wrong, mister?'

He came out of it slowly, couldn't reply until the knotting left his guts.

'Nice place,' he got out.

'Nice? That's like saying Jefferson Davis was an all right President! Come on, you can do better than that.'

He might have but for the fact that an even stronger emotion than simple envy was suddenly working on him now. It was a feeling too strong to be dismissed, a warning that told him not to go one step closer to Rand Braden's earthly paradise, drowsing there in the fading crimson light, that to do so would surely cost him dear.

He shook his head. He was a practical man who had no faith in presentiments, omens or premonitions.

He heeled his horse forward. The cattleman studied his face curiously as he rode past him and led him down the curving gravel driveway to the ornate iron gates to the Buffalo Gate.

A soft chiming of spurs, the screech of gate-hinges, and the gamy smell of an unwashed body heralded the arrival of Balthazar at the adobe home of Miguel Sanchez.

'Hey, *amigo*!' the man shouted in the darkness. 'Are you hiding in there?'

A tall shape stirred in the gloom of the darkened porch.

'What do you want, Bal?'

The new arrival mounted the steps and peered at the lean figure in the battered old chair.

'The *señor* is back, Miguel.'

'I know it.'

'He has a new *hombre* with him.'

'This also I know.'

'You are not disturbed?'

'I am disturbed. And I wish to be alone.'

'It shall be as you say, Miguel,' the man replied and left immediately, heading down the line of houses that comprised the Mexican riders' village on Buffalo Gate.

Sanchez sighed as he reached for a cigar. Why did they always come to him? It was always the same, whether a man was killed by a fall from a horse, or a baby had the belly-ache. They always expected he would know what should be done. They were like children, and since the days when the patron had

44

gone from this place, they had made him their father. Sometimes he welcomed all this responsibility, but at other times, like tonight, it burdened him.

The ramrod of Buffalo Gate put a light to a cigar and leaned back, exhaling slowly as he gazed out over the rapidly darkening landscape before him.

He sighed.

Before the Alamo and the Little Big Horn, before the iron teeth of the railroads chewed through the Great West, and before the madness they called the War Between The States, all this had belonged to his people.

Just how long the people from the South with their music, culture, their pride and their strong stone churches had owned this country, nobody seemed really to know.

Then came the gringos.

The early arrivals were lean and bearded madmen, mad for gold, for furs, for Spanish women and for adventure. Then came the true Americans whose only interest was in the land, and they took by force or by trickery the lands of Pancho Guiterrez and those of Manuel Torredo. They took the old grants and broke them up and fought over them, then guarded the things they had stolen with their long guns.

In time squatters and thieves became respectable *rancheros*, who hired the former kings of the range-lands to accept a roof over their heads and a bellyful of oat mash at night in return for days spent in the saddle from dawn till dark. Used the whip on those who made trouble. For those who continued to make trouble – shot them.

Viva America!

The tall man leaned and spat. Until he'd learned better, Miguel Sanchez had spiritually shared the burden of every dispossessed Mexican north of the Rio. Not any longer. Only this land, once bearing the proud name of Rancho Antigua, was his concern now. This was his earth, his sky, his future – at least in his heart.

But what of this tall gringo Braden had brought back with him? Sanchez had met the man named Dev, spoken with him and felt his strength in their handshake. There was mystery in the man also, he felt, a sense that was deepened by the fact that he only proffered the single name: 'Dev'.

'Found a new hand for you, ramrod,' Braden had said offhandedly. But if tall and fair-haired Dev actually proved to be just another range rider, then his foreman was no judge.

Friend or foe?

Only time would tell. Only time would determine whether the hated Braden's new gringo would accept the ramrod's hand in true friendship, or fill the grave of an enemy. On Buffalo Gate, in the realm of Miguel Sanchez's ambition, it could only be one thing or the other.

CHAPTER 4

EVALINA

Handyman Pas was deeply impressed.

'The gringo has great skill.'

'If the gringo didn't learn the skill the gringo's house would have fallen in on him,' Dev grinned. 'You watching?'

'*Sí.*'

Dev glanced towards the house below as he picked up his chalkline. Following breakfast at the cookhouse, he'd gone up to the house only to be told that Braden was occupied. So he found an occupation for himself when he went to see what the ranch carpenter was doing on his trestles, and had set about helping him hew a couple of planks.

First he rubbed the chalkline with fresh chalk, then fitted it to a bitch in one end of the log. Dev drew the string tighter along the timber on the line he wished to cut, then snapped it with his finger, leaving a long straight line of chalk dust upon the surface of the wood.

Old Pas watched in awe as he took up a light scor-
ing-axe and scored the timber down the line to the
depth of a quarter-inch. This was to give the broadaxe something to bite into when he began squaring.
Grabbing up a broadaxe now, he came down on the
scored line at an angle that took a thin slab off the
side of the log, exactly as timbermen did it with a saw
in the mill. He struck hard enough just to carry the
blade through, then with an up-and-down motion of
the handle, took the slab off right down the line.

After he had hewn one side, he turned the log
over to work the other, taking less than five minutes
to produce a perfectly hewn plank.

The ancient retainer was deeply impressed.

'*Madre*! Where do you learn such things, Señor
Dev?'

His smile was almost grim.

'You pick up a little here, a little there . . .' His
voice drifted.

He was admiring his surroundings again. The
more he saw of Buffalo Gate the finer it appeared.
Today he was seeing it in contrast with his four
sections of dry Flint River dirt, so far from this
verdant chunk of the territory.

It didn't seem to do him any good to be thinking
that way.

Sounds reached him from the great house. He
glanced across green lawns, shaded patios, meticu-
lously tended gardens to the gleaming windows. The
big man would see him when he felt good and ready,
he reckoned. And why should it be otherwise?
Braden was king here and he just a commoner, if

48

even that high up the scale.

The hands had left for the round-up an hour earlier, but there was any amount of work going on round the headquarters.

Across at the corrals, which were shielded from the house by a line of great blue cedars, three *vaqueros* were breaking in a long-legged bay gelding, blood horse by the looks. He could see a man working in the orchard, hacking at deadwood with a hatchet. A plump maid emerged from a side door of the great house to hurry along the long portico with an armful of linen.

His gaze sharpened. As he followed the maid's progress, he saw a pale face gazing from a window hung with gold-trimmed curtains of heavy brocade. The young woman appeared to be watching him steadily, without expression. The house was fifty yards distant and the window lay in shadow, yet even so he could see it was a beautiful face, heart-shaped and vivid, framed by hair as black as midnight.

Vallery set the ladle down, wiped his mouth with the back of his hand and walked back from the pump to the carpenter who was making a king-sized botch of his hewing job.

'Always cut a little away from the scoring, Pas.'

'I cut.'

Dev glanced over his shoulder. The face was still there.

'Like so, *amigo* Dev?'

He inspected the cut and frowned.

'Who's that at the window, Pas?'

The Mexican squinted at the house.

'Ah, the old eyes are no longer sharp, but I would know the *señora* clear across the valley.'

'*Señora?*'

'Mrs Braden.'

'That's Braden's wife?'

'*Sí.* You seem surprised, Señor Dev.'

'Well, mebbe I am. It's just that she looks so young.'

'She is young ... not yet twenty-one.' Gregorio sighed. 'Young and sad. Is not like the other *señora*. She was big and strong and—'

'What other *señora?*'

'The Mrs Braden who died when the blackwater fever struck last summer. This Mrs Braden, she has been here on the Buffalo Gate some three years but I think it seems much longer for her.'

'Why do you say that?'

Gregorio dropped his gaze.

'I think maybe I talk too much. I think maybe I just watch while you teach me more with the axe.'

Dev shrugged and went back to work. He was tempted to snatch a glance at the window but let it go. He was about through with his second plank when a shadow fell across the log. He looked up sharply; he'd heard no approaching steps. A man stood before him, a slab-faced giant with a crooked back and huge hands almost reaching to his knees.

'Vallery.' The voice that came out of the huge body was toneless. 'Mr Braden wants you at the house.'

'Who are you?' he demanded.

'This is Yancey, Mr Braden's man,' Gregorio

supplied. 'You should hurry, Señor Dev. Señor Braden does not like to wait.'

Vallery nodded. So this was the house-guard. The *vaqueros* had warned he would be surprised when he saw him, and they weren't wrong.

'All right, Yancey,' he said. 'Let's go.'

The man didn't speak as they crossed the sunny yard, and Vallery noted that, despite his bulk, the man was surprisingly light on his feet. He moved like a wrestler, he thought, and judging by the massive thews would be a hard man to toss in the ring.

They entered the house and Yancey showed him into a vast room, then left without a sound.

Vallery gaped.

The twenty-by-twenty room was cool and shaded although the morning was already quite warm. It was richly furnished in Spanish style, with a long desk of polished cedar, twin scarlet sofas with rolled ends, chairs in red-and-gold brocade that looked like Mexico to him, even if he'd never been there. Scarlet-and-gold tapestries adorned the walls. As he moved about, his boots sank into deep carpeting that muffled his spurs. He was building a cigarette some time later when a light step sounded in the hallway. He turned, expecting to see Braden, but instead found himself staring at the same striking face he'd seen in the window.

The woman appeared startled on seeing him.

'Oh, I didn't know there was anybody here.'

'Mrs Braden,' he said formally. 'I'm Dev.'

'Of course. My husband told me about you. Welcome to Buffalo Gate, Mr Dev.'

'Just Dev, ma'am.' His cigarette was forgotten. He knew he was staring. Young and somehow wild-looking, she was tall and lithe with budding breasts outlined by a yellow silk blouse. Her unusual eyes were of the most brilliant jade green; she had a short tip-tilted nose and a delicate flowerlike mouth. How could any poor sodbuster, jailbird, fugitive do anything but stare?

They made small talk. He admired her house. In return she declared herself both pleased and relieved that her husband seemed to have found in him the right-hand man he needed so badly.

He hung on to that, digested it. Sure, Braden had seemed excited to have secured his services – doubly so upon discovering he was a wanted criminal. He realized Mr Big needed to have an American he could trust on the spread to keep an eye on his crew, yet was still puzzled why a man in his position would go out of his way to hire a man wanted by the law.

But, of course, he had realized back in Muleshoe that Rand Braden was anything but an everyday kind of operator.

Braden appeared suddenly in the doorway, dressed for riding in dungarees and a tailored dark-blue shirt that emphasized his hard, muscular build. Had everything, Dev remembered thinking later. Looks, strength, money, success, gorgeous young wife. But he must still have problems, otherwise he'd never have hired someone like himself.

'I'm sure you have duties to occupy you elsewhere, Evalina,' he said.

'Of course, Rand.' She smiled at Vallery as she

turned to go. 'It was pleasant meeting you, Dev. I . . . I hope you stay.' She sounded as if she meant it.

She left. Her husband frowned as he crossed to the desk. He sat and reached for the cigar humidor.

'You can stop drooling, mister.'

'Drooling?' Dev snapped. 'What the hell are you talking about?'

Braden leaned back and fired up the big Corona jammed between his teeth.

'You take me for a fool, mister? I saw the way you looked at her – the same way everyone does. Well, you can cut it out if you—'

'That's enough!'

'What . . .'

Vallery jabbed a finger at him, jaws tight and hard.

'Look, Braden, you might like to think you're God almighty here, but nobody talks to me that way. If I was looking at your wife in any special way it's because she's beautiful, as you damn well know, and because she has manners, which you don't. I know I might be beholden to you, mister, and sure, you can do me a lot of harm if you've a mind. But if you reckon that gives you the edge to walk over me, you'd better think again. So, if you don't like what I'm saying, why don't you get up out of that fat chair and do something about it?'

Everything was silent for a long moment, conflicting emotions chasing one another across Braden's powerful face. At length he shrugged.

'Maybe I was a bit outspoken at that, Dev.'

'Not maybe – were.'

'Forgotten.' Braden spread his hands. 'But what a

man can get away with once here, doesn't mean he can do it twice. You better remember . . .' He paused with a frown. 'What are you looking at?'

'You've got callused hands.'

'So?'

Vallery shrugged, but was puzzled. He knew plenty about calluses from a lifetime of hard work and a rock-breaking stint behind bars.

'Just never pictured you working with your hands, somehow,' he said defensively.

Braden's smile was knowing; he was pleased.

'Uh-huh. Well, let me tell you something, mister. You're not the only one who came up the hard way. I've busted my back and ridden the range and day-labored in places likely tougher than you've ever seen. Difference between you and me is that I had something up here.'

He tapped his temple.

'You kept busting your back because that was as far as you could see ahead. Me? I had my eye on the main chance from the get-go, and when I saw it, I grabbed it.' He leaned back. 'Guess now you're start-ing to understand why I'm on this side of the desk and you're over there.'

Vallery just nodded. He'd been told, and it hurt because he sensed it might be true. He shrugged, concentrated on his cigarette, but both knew Braden had scored the clincher. Dev was jealous, maybe for the first time in his life. He recognized the fact, didn't care for it one damn bit.

Braden rose. Having won the hand, he felt he could afford to be generous.

'I'm not always this ornery,' he said, standing at the huge windows. 'The truth is, things didn't go so well while I was absent looking for . . . you, as it turned out.'

'In what way?'

'The round-up's way behind schedule. That's my main gripe.'

'It's still early in the season.'

Braden swung to face him.

'It suits me to muster early every season to drive our stock to the railhead at Fort James. Buffalo Gate cows always fetch top dollar, but not if too much rubbish gets delivered ahead of us. Early on, the buyers are eager and looking for quality. But once they get snowed under with volume, they take a tougher line and the prices come down. So . . . I get there early. *Sabe?*'

'Let me guess. You want me to work with the men and move things along.'

'Smart.' Braden grinned. 'Knew I'd picked the right man.' He sobered. 'Sure, that's what I want. But watch your step, mister. There's a lot of hate on this place, especially if you grow yellow whiskers and don't wear a sombrero. People get hurt on the Gate, but I don't want you to be one of them. Am I making myself clear?'

'I guess.'

'Done.'

Braden strode round the desk, grabbed up a pen and began to write. It took Dev a moment to realize he'd been dismissed.

He was half-smiling as he walked out into the corridor and followed it through to the flagged patio.

Sunlight bouncing off whitewashed walls was an assault to the eyes after the cool gloom of the interior. As he strode along the pathway through the gardens, he imagined he felt the weight of watching eyes boring into his back. He halted and turned.

Yancey stood by the tankstand, the lower half of him in shadow. The giant seemed to be doing nothing in particular, just watching him with expressionless eyes. Vallery was about to move on when he glimpsed the face at the window again. He nodded and saluted. She didn't return his gesture yet her eyes appeared to be trying to communicate something. He shook his head and headed on for the stables. Imagination, Vallery, he chided himself. It's not your style to get fanciful ideas just because you see a pretty face.

The livery boy helped him saddle his buckskin and told him the shortest route to the Two Mile. He rode out in brilliant sunshine and didn't look back until passing through the main gates.

Braden's wife was still watching him.

So, too, was the giant with the crooked back.

Why?

The bellowing of the cattle echoed back from the tree-line that flanked the flat lands at Two Mile Sink as the *vaqueros* pushed the gather towards the marshalling yards. The animals were parched from the drive and had caught the smell of water coming from the sink. A flock of jaybirds rose out of the trees, screeching in annoyance as the cattle approached.

It was a mile from the timber to the water and the

stock crossed it at a ragged trot. There were roughly fifty in the bunch, baldy-faced young steers, fat cows and young dogies bleating behind. The cattle, most of them half-wild from roaming the ranges all winter on the southern graze, had been flushed out of canyons and brush-choked draws by eagle-eyed horsemen who now spurred on ahead in order to slow them down so that none would get trampled as they rushed in to drink.

Vallery swabbed sweat from his neck with his bandanna as he reined in by the sink and watched the cattle drink. Sanchez hadn't been here when he arrived from the house, so he'd promptly pitched in and helped the cowboys bring them in over the last five miles. They had neither welcomed him nor shown any hostility. He was content with that. They already knew he had Braden's authority behind him, and that would be enough for now.

He turned his head to watch Rilla come splashing across the sink on his ugly cow pony. The hawk-faced Mexican with the bitter black eyes and a reckless dash of a mustache assumed charge in the ramrod's absence. The man shot him a cold stare, then rode on to the group behind and ordered them to chow down at the chuck wagon while they had the chance.

Dev followed slowly, aware of the furtive stares as he swung down, looped his lines over a branch, then crossed to the chuck wagon. He picked up a tin dish and approached the sullen cook.

'What's good, *amigo*?'

The bulky man stared, spat, then said grudgingly: 'Beans.'

'If that's the menu – I guess I'll have beans.'

'You want beans, you get beans.'

He studied the man. He was big and strong-looking. The camp had gone quiet. Seated in the sparse shade in a semicircle, the crew were no longer eating, but watching. They appeared expectant. This was plainly some kind of test.

'Fill my plate.'

A shrug of heavy shoulders was his only answer. Somebody sniggered.

'Did you hear me, joker?'

'I serve *amigos*, not gringos.'

'You don't get the notion. I'm not asking, I'm telling. Fill this plate.'

'No!'

Vallery shrugged to disguise what was coming. His right hand whipped out and his hard slap across the cheek sounded across the sink sharp as a gunshot. The cook's eyes rolled whitely and he swung wildly with his heavy ladle. Dev ducked under it, blocked the fast punch that followed with his shoulder, then pistoned a perfectly timed right straight to the point. The man's eyes glazed over, he stared at him sightlessly across his bench, then went slowly over backwards like building collapsing.

The silence was profound as a dozen *vaqueros* stared at one of their best sprawled on his back in the dust like something crucified. Then everyone began jabbering at once, the racket concealing the sound of fast approaching hoofbeats. Vallery was helping himself to the stew when the authoritative voice cracked out.

'You!'

Vallery turned to see Miguel Sanchez striding towards him.

'Howdy.'

Vallery continued filling his plate. The two had met briefly the night before, a chilly meeting. Sanchez acted suspicious of Braden's new signing. In turn, Vallery had been told the ramrod was the best man on the place but possibly too popular, too strong and 'ambitious', whatever the man had meant by that.

'I wouldn't get my tail in a crack over this if I was you, Sanchez,' he advised, turning and fingering a chunk of stew meat from the plate. 'He wouldn't serve me. Maybe he will next time.'

It seemed a long uncertain time before the foreman turned slowly to stare at the hands, black brows hooked up like twin question marks. Eventually the hawkish Rilla stopped picking his teeth with a match.

'Perhaps it happens as the gringo says, Miguel,' he said.

Sanchez expelled a ragged breath.

'Then . . . so be it . . .' Then he straightened and his voice snapped sharp. 'Clean up this mess and shift those cattle away before they bloat. *Arriba! Arriba!*'

Vallery nodded in approval as hands jumped to obey. He studied the ramrod with increased respect. Miguel could have made an issue of the incident, but the fellow was plainly smart enough to realize Vallery was within his rights. After a while he strolled across to where the sweating Sanchez had hunkered down on his spurs in the sparse shade of a sapling to sip cold coffee from a battered pannikin.

'I do not care for trouble on the job, *señor*.'

'I'm not much for it myself.'

The man squinted up at him. 'You fight well. The cook is strong.'

'Lucky punch.'

'And yesterday, when you shot the eagle at long distance. Also lucky?'

'You seem to have something on your mind, Sanchez.'

The ramrod rose. He was as tall as Vallery, with unusually powerful arms for a lean man. There were scars on his face, part of an eyebrow was missing. A formidable fighting face.

'I believe I should know whom I am working with.'

'I'm just a hand. Didn't Braden tell you?'

The man's face shadowed. '*Sí*, he told me.' He was silent for a time, weighing Vallery with his eyes. 'Very well, we shall let the matter rest. But next time there is trouble you will come to me.'

'You're the ramrod.'

'This is so. And now, to make certain there is no further trouble today, you shall work with me.'

'Whatever you say, boss man.'

CHAPTER 5

AMBUSCADE

The second shot sounded even louder than the first and Vallery heard the brutal smack of the bullet ploughing into the tree-trunk inches above his head as he plunged from his saddle, rolled violently, then kicked into the grassy swale.

Silence.

He lay frozen, listening to the thudding of his heart and aware of the cold sweat across his forehead.

That had been close!

A short distance away he heard his horse slow and then halt. In his mind's eye he saw the buckskin rolling its gaze back at the tree, looking for him, intensely alert for more gunfire.

Dev stared at the yellow moon and it stared back, cold and uncaring. He cautiously stretched all four limbs in turn to make certain he wasn't hit; he was in one piece. He spat cotton, took a fresh grip on the Winchester then bellied forward across the swale, moving in the direction the shot had come from. He figured he was three miles south-east of the Gate headquarters and close by the old line-rider's shack hard by the cattle trail.

A week after signing on with Buffalo Gate he'd fallen into the habit of taking the short cut back from the round-up site, cutting across Blue Knob, then picking up the old trail here and following it back to home.

Five days of hostility, tension, a hell of a lot of work and a few fresh calluses. But, up until now, no real trouble.

A dry-gulcher was trouble enough for any man.

He raised his head with infinite caution. The adobe building lay directly ahead, silent and still in its black patches of moonshadow.

A window blinked at him.

Vallery couldn't see what caused the momentary interruption to the reflected moonsheen on that window. But natural smarts and a wealth of experience enabled him to make an educated guess. Something, about man-height, had passed along the deeply shadowed gallery.

It could only be the low son of a bitch who'd tried to kill him.

He was white-hot angry and intent on getting in close with his Winchester. But he was restrained for a long moment by a clawing uncertainty. What if it was the law, hunting convicted 'man-killer' Dev Vallery? Or worse, some low bounty hunter who would just as happily take him in dead as alive?

Calmer reasoning prevailed. He must be realistic.

He must be safer here than at any time since his escape. And would any lawman or manhunter risk invading a heavily armed cattle ranch where trouble was running high and they had look-outs with Winchester .32s posted all over against rustlers?

Not likely.

He rolled backwards and quit the recess under cover of a line of blue sage shrubs which took him chancelessly down to the barn in back of the house on its northern side.

By this he was ice-cold calm and deliberate as a hanging judge. The house and outbuildings showed no sign of life, at first. Then a faint brief spurt of match flame behind a blackened window told him where his man was: second room from the right end by the chimney.

He threw his rifle to his shoulder and began triggering with a slow, steady rhythm. For a long handful of seconds the little valley rocked to the insane smash of rapid fire mingled with the tinkling of shattered glass and falling objects within the building which seemed to shudder from the impact of his brutal volley.

Gunsmoke wreathed thickly just above ground-level as he sprang to his feet and zigzagged down-slope. He discarded the empty Winchester and produced the Peacemaker as distance whipped behind him.

A single shot came searching as a headlong dive carried him ten feet through the air to hit and roll behind the natural cover of the hump of ground flanking the rusted pump.

The slug rang off the pump-handle. He must be up against a molly-duffer with a gun!

Boosted by this realization he bucked to his feet and darted to the safety of the corner of the house, a muffled curse of frustration from within telling him that the advantage – all the dry-gulcher's way initially, had just exchanged hands.

He now knew where his man was, while the dry-gulcher could only guess at his position. Ace against Deuce.

He cat-footed around the end of the house, then drew himself up to full height by the galley window. Inside, someone was tiptoeing across a creaky floor. Bending low, Dev scrabbled round for a pebble and flicked it to hit the partially opened rear door.

Yellow gunflashes lit the interior as the man triggered back, and by their light he sensed rather than saw the bulky silhouette.

The window pane shivered into a blizzard of fragments as he blasted through it twice, his second shot rewarded by a gasp of pure agony, the crash of a falling body.

He kicked the door in and hurled himself to one side. But nobody was trying to kill him now. The dark figure on the floor was moaning softly; '*Dios mio . . . Dios mio . . .*'

Vallery kicked the dropped revolver away and seized him by the collar to drag him out on to the back porch.

It was the cook from the round-up camp. The one, he learned later, called Benito.

*

64

'I've got bad news, Mex. Looks like you're going to live.'

'Your mother is a—'

His kick chopped off the wounded man's words. He slapped him hard across the face, then paradoxically, bent to adjust the sling he'd just fitted to his wounded arm.

'Tell me, why, Mex,' he growled. 'That's the only chance you've got. Clam up, and I'll take you into the law in Fort James and charge you with attempted murder. What's it to be?'

The wounded man had no way of knowing that Dev Vallery would not go within a mile of a law office even should his life depend upon it. The man had been high on bravado earlier. Now there was a chill in the air, he was hurting bad, and the man called Dev appeared at least angry and dangerous enough to carry out his threat.

Benito was a tough man who expected no mercy. Tough enough to keep silent even when his life was on the line, maybe, yet something stronger worked against this. He needed to speak, to air his grievances.

'You are the enemy, *señor*. That is why I shoot. I wished to kill you before you killed us . . .'

'What are you talking about, back-shooter? I'm nobody's enemy here. I only returned fire when you opened up on me like a yellow dog.' He racheted back the hammer of his long-barrelled pistol and angled it downwards at Benito's thick gut. 'And the more I think on that . . .'

He was bluffing but the other wasn't to know that.

'Go ahead, *señor*.' The Mexican seemed to discover a fatalistic pride in what he'd done, a defiance. 'Better you kill me now than I hang.'

That last word hit the American hard. He was still angry but his pistol no longer menaced the other as he backed up a step.

'Why did you try to kill me?'

'I already say. You are the *señor*'s man, so you will bring harm to us.'

'You realize what the law can do to you?'

Benito managed a sneer. His wound didn't appear to be too serious.

'Law? The law will not deal with Benito.'

'What do you mean by that? If I report—'

'I might hang, but not at the hands of the law. Señor Braden does not deal with the law. The *señor* is the law on the *rancho*.'

Vallery's anger was receding as he began pacing to and fro.

'Keep talking,' he ordered, wondering why he wanted to hear more of what a would-be assassin thought about his employer, of himself.

For an illiterate range cook, Benito had plenty of opinions and seeming facts to support them. The picture he painted of Braden was an ugly one. He insisted that the big man had stolen the former Rancho Antiguo from its owners through legal trickery supported by hired 'gringo gangs' which had intimidated, beaten and even murdered in the name of Braden's concept of American expansion into the south-west.

He claimed Miguel Sanchez to be the true legal

owner of Buffalo Gate while at the same time conceding that Braden's grip was now too powerful ever to be broken. He said that Sanchez 'dreamed' of recovering what he believed was rightly his but in reality was resigned to never rising higher than ramrod on 'his' land.

'If a man has enough money, can grease enough palms, hire enough crooked attorneys and pay enough of the right bribes to the right people in the Lands Office, then Waterquick County is his paradise. Many of the old Spanish land grants are poorly worded, and can be picked apart by Yankee buzzards, like picking the carcass. This is what befalls the sad Miguel, what burdens him while he works for almost nothing for the man who ruined him. . . .'

The longer he spoke the more confident and passionate Benito the cook became, although how much was true and how much simple resentment and bitterness Dev could only guess.

In the man's eyes, Braden was evil incarnate, who, he claimed, 'might have had something to do with his first wife's death, and who was rumored to have literally bought his current wife somewhere south of the border. He even conjured up a price; the equivalent of $10,000 in US currency.

Vallery stared at the man.

'What foolishness is this, damnit? You're talking slavery, you understand?'

The dark head bobbed.

'We shirtless ones know all about slavery, gringo.'

'You expect me to believe that a man like Braden, who entertains the biggest people in the territory,

67

and is pals with the governor – who could likely get any woman he wanted legitimately, would buy a woman like you would a horse? It's crazy!'

'The Señor Braden is not like other men. You have been here long enough to realize that.' Benito winced and adjusted his shoulder-strapping. Then his look turned sly. 'Then there is the *señora* herself, gringo. You have seen her beauty. Would not any man buy such loveliness if he was given but one small chance. . . ?'

At this point Vallery sensed that a combination of pain, the whiskey he was feeding the fellow and his obvious bitterness towards his employer might be getting the better of Benito. It was late, the man needed attention, a decision had to be made.

'Look, frypan, if I agreed to put this foolishness of yours tonight down to bad temper and stupidity and agree not to report it to either the law or Braden, would you be prepared to swear you won't try anything like that on me again?'

Benito's eyes looked huge as saucers. There were sudden tears. 'Why would you do this? You play with Benito? I tried to murder you.'

'Answer me.' Dev's mind was racing ahead. He saw how this ugly business could be papered over. He wanted that. He was even half-sorry for the cook by this. But more significantly, he didn't want to set anything in train that might attract unwanted attention from the law, which could just possibly result in a certain Fort James lawman showing up on the Gate and maybe taking an unwanted interest in one Dev Vallery.

'Would you swear?'

Benito nodded so vigorously and wept so convincingly that Dev decided he was worth the risk.

Riding on to the village through the moonshadows, he framed his story in his mind: Benito had shot himself accidentally cleaning his rifle. Vallery had come across him and escorted him home. No questions, no suspicions; just an everyday kind of accident that could happen to anyone.

Benito kissed his hands and promised to name his first son after him when they parted company at the ranch's Mexican village.

Dev Vallery rode home slowly and for once in his fugitive life had something more than himself and simple survival to occupy his thoughts.

'More caviar, Dev?'

'Er, not right now.'

'A little rich for the palate?'

'I guess.'

Braden smiled at his wife seated at the far end of the huge oak table which seemed in danger of sagging beneath the weight of flowers, food, candelabra and fine vintages.

'Of course you will have another helping, my dear?' He winked across at Vallery. 'Evalina was born to the silk, you know. Ah yes, her ancestors date back almost to Cortés. She knows all manner of interesting people, has been to the most fascinating places ... haven't you, my dear? Now what about you, Miguel? More red wine, perhaps?'

'*Sí*, Señor Braden.'

The ramrod kept glancing across at Dev, who wasn't sure whether Sanchez believed the story of Benito's bullet wound.

Discreet servants bustled about and Vallery watched it all without quite believing it.

The Buffalo Gate ranch house was the first great hacienda he'd ever seen from the inside. From the outset he'd been deeply impressed, envious but impressed as seldom before. But this supper which Braden had announced at short notice made him fully appreciate the hugeness of the gap separating his employer from normal everyday folks. And that surely went double or treble for a killer on the run.

Golden goblets, diamonds at the woman's throat, fantastic foods and sweetmeats imported from God alone knew where.

And presiding over it all as though to the manor born, Rand Braden, looking every inch as though he had never known anything different.

Yet he knew Braden had clawed his way up to this dizzy height, while Dev Vallery had been lucky to keep body and soul together.

The two men began talking cows, leaving Dev and Evalina to make small talk. He was fine with that. Although not overtly a ladies' man, he admired beautiful women and Evalina Braden had that category sewn up, hand-delivered and personally patented. But along with perfect features and a bright and intense personality, Braden's young Mexican wife possessed some unexpected quality or characteristic that he couldn't put a name to, at least not yet. Whatever it might be, it just served to make the woman more attractive and somehow mysterious.

Maybe 'mysterious' was the word he was searching for?

'It was very kind of you to come to the cook's assistance the other night, Dev,' she smiled. 'After his accident, I mean. Mrs Latimer told me today that Benito is quickly recovering.'

At mention of the housekeeper's name he found himself probing the shadows beyond the table-lights for sign of the woman. Then he saw her silhouette by the servery door and, a short distance away, leaning crookedly like some grotesque carving, the unnerving Yancey.

'Glad to hear it,' he said.

She lowered her voice. 'You should know that my husband does not care for that surly cook.'

'Uh-huh.' He was delighted to be talking with her but would be happy to leave Benito out of it.

Evalina leaned back and sipped delicately from her glass.

'Rand believes Benito hates him, and is suspicious concerning how he came by his injury.'

This time he just nodded, was surprised when the woman giggled.

'But that is nothing to worry about. My husband thinks all the *vaqueros* hate him and are plotting to one day disembowel him and feed his intestines to the vultures. Do you not think that strange?'

He was aware he'd spilled a little of his drink. Maybe he didn't consider workers hating their employer all that strange; what hit him as odd was her phrasing and choice of words. It was almost, he thought, as though she found the prospect of her husband meeting such a gruesome end somehow amusing. Her words were so unexpected, her dimpled smile so innocent, in truth, that for a moment he wasn't sure as he'd heard right.

But studying her closely as she turned to issue instructions to the sweets maid, he knew he had. He realized she was plainly fully aware of the effects her words might have, while at the same time could obviously not care less.

When she next met his eye he momentarily saw beyond the dreamily beautiful heart-shaped face and sparkling Spanish eyes to glimpse something he'd not seen before. For just a moment, Evalina Braden was not the faultless hostess but rather some offbeat creature with a glitter in her eye that was part flirtatiousness, part tempered steel.

It was as though he'd been afforded a glimpse of the woman beneath the wife in a way that might have been deliberate, or could just as probably be accidental.

Then the ramrod was speaking.

'Do you intend to occupy the *señora*'s attention all night, Dev?'

He knew he was glad of Sanchez's interruption, and as ramrod and ranch-mistress engaged in easy chatter, he rose to fill a chair at Braden's side, where he accepted a fresh full glass.

Braden was a torrent of eager talk about round-ups, beef prices, train schedules, and 'loafing, lousy Mex hands'. Vallery was content to let him run with the conversational ball. It was one full week since he'd ridden on to the great *rancho* and he was feeling, if not actually totally secure, then at least increasingly comfortable and at ease. He'd picked up quickly on the rhythm of the ranch and had established his worth, with his ranching skills and knowledge of the beef business. He nightly reported to Braden on anything and everything which he felt the rancher might want to hear about. But apart from the 'accident' befalling Benito the cook, there had been little enough to pass on.

Sometimes he fretted that he might look up from a red-hot branding-iron one day to see the funereal features and gaunt grey shape of Marshal Kells, yet Buffalo Gate continued to feel as safe a haven to a desperate man as he might ever hope to find.

Their conversation was interrupted when Sanchez slapped his thigh at some joke and Evalina's laughter filled the room.

Suddenly the rancher was sober again as he touched the tip of a cigar to a candle and drew deeply.

'What do you think of my wife, *fugitivo?*'

Vallery was taken aback as much by the other's use of the word as the question itself. He blanked his expression and adjusted the bandanna he'd borrowed in an attempt to improve his attire for the occasion.

'She's . . . quite beautiful. . . .'

'But the question is – should a cat look at a queen?'

He suspected the boss man had likely taken one rich red too many.

73

'Reckon I don't understand the question.'

'I saw you drooling, mister. Just as my ramrod is doing now.'

'Nothing wrong with a good drool, I always say.'

'Don't cut wise with me, rope-dodger—'

'Why don't you holler so the whole place hears?' Vallery snapped back. 'What's got into you, anyway? You've got a beautiful wife yet you don't expect anyone to admire her? How dumb is that?'

For a moment he thought he'd gone too far. Braden seemed to pale, then shrugged and cracked his knuckles. But when he spoke his voice was controlled again even though his mood was bitter now.

'I guess I'm tetchy on account I'm getting more and more suspicious of Miguel every day, mister. He's fiery and passionate by nature, yet with me he's always respectful and obedient, almost meek. I don't trust that. I hear whispers, such as that he has connections with *bandidos* in the mountains, that he plans to put me under the ground with their help and that of every treacherous greaser son of a bitch on this place. I wouldn't be surprised if he'd not stop at trying to poison my own wife against me . . .'

'If you feel that way,' Vallery said, rising, 'why not fire him?'

'What? And have the conspiracy against me just go underground? No. That man is working up to something and I want to know what it is. You know I've set it up for you to ride with him tomorrow? Very well. You work on him – I think he half-trusts you. Cozy up, be a pal, hint that you hate my guts and would

74

like the chance to do something about it. I don't care
what you do, only bring me back something.'

Dev just nodded, made no reply.

Later, making his goodnights, he took the young
wife's hand and she stood on tiptoes and kissed him
fully on the mouth while Braden was discussing
something with the ramrod.

He walked alone downslope in the moonlight to
the long adobe bunkhouse he shared with the *vaqueros* of the Buffalo Gate, yet after he'd gone maybe
half-way he felt impelled to stop and turn.

Lights were dimming in the hacienda yet it
seemed to him the place was surrounded by some
kind of aura which might have stemmed from the
beauty and age of the building itself, or be due to the
people he'd seen here tonight.

There was Braden with his rich man's arrogance
and all his fears, Sanchez, the strong man apparently
subservient to his boss, the housekeeper who
appeared to see and hear everything yet said very
little, the strong man watching the wife, Evalina
herself, maybe the hardest to read of all.

Small wonder that when he turned his back again
he felt a strange tingling between his shoulder
blades, like a warning signal. It was that sort of house,
that sort of people. Maybe if he stayed here long
enough he might get to understand why he should
feel this way.

CHAPTER 6

CAME A GREY RIDER

They rode away across the sloping mesa that stretched east to west of Two Mile Sink. The vastness of the Buffalo Gate range impressed as always, and Vallery wondered if it was envy again causing him to think . . . *Too much of everything for just one man . . . .*

Miguel Sanchez rode at his side, sitting his ornate saddle with the ease of the born rider. The ramrod was around his own age, he guessed, maybe a year or two older. The blood of his Spanish ancestry showed clearly in the handsome, sculpted features and the lean, straight-backed lines of his body. Gregorio the handyman had insisted that just about every female in fifty miles had eyes for Sanchez, and he supposed he could believe it.

He guessed he quite liked the fellow, but like so many denizens of this cattle empire, the ramrod appeared reserved and secretive, as though he was nursing some mystery.

They spent the afternoon running strays out of the brush. Once they'd rounded up a bunch they would haze them off to the nearest working party, then scout off looking for more. In all they mustered thirty-three head before Sanchez decided they'd done enough for one day.

Sunset was approaching by the time the ramrod finished giving instructions to the hands regarding the nighthawk duties at Two Mile Sink. Only then did they cut north-east, heading back for headquarters.

'Ever see country this fine?' Sanchez said casually as they swept past a tiny spring circled by willows trailing their green fingers in the crystal water.

'Can't say I have.'

They covered another mile in silence before Sanchez drew his flashy black to a halt atop a high bluff. The soft red sunlight was dying on the western slopes of the grassy swells which rolled away from them like the waves of the sea.

'Twenty thousand acres sure covers a heap of territory,' Vallery drawled, hands busy with tobacco and papers. 'A whole lot of dirt for just one man,' he added deliberately.

He sensed the other's sharp glance. After a long silence the Mexican said quietly: 'Some might say it is far too much, Señor Dev.'

Vallery drew on his cigarette and let the smoke trickle from his lips. He watched the limitless pink wash of the fading day become a dusk of purple shadows and a mystic softness.

'Do you reckon it's overmuch land for one man, Miguel?'

'A Mexican is not supposed to think.'

'Not supposed to, mebbe . . . but you do, don't you.'

'Maybe . . .' the man replied, his eyes full of secrets, the hint of unleashed power in his lean length as his senses fed on what he was seeing, feeling. Studying him, Vallery was suddenly curious to know more about him, whether for Braden's benefit or to satisfy his own curiosity, he wasn't sure. Of course Braden had told him plenty about Miguel, but Vallery had lived too long to believe all he was told. 'How much are you paid, Sanchez?' he asked bluntly.

The other's black eyes snapped at him.

'That is a personal matter. Why do you ask?'

'Just curious. I know he pays the hands just fifteen a month. So I calculate twenty would be about top for you.'

'And if this was so?'

'You're a top hand, know your cattle, handle men just fine. A man with your ability could draw sixty or seventy a month 'most anyplace else. Why do you stick it here?'

He was sure he knew the answer. But sure wasn't certain.

Sanchez's eyes glittered. Had Vallery not already assessed this outwardly compliant ranch hand as a hard and possibly dangerous man, his expression then would have confirmed it.

'Did Braden tell you to ask me that?' the man demanded.

'No. But I'm still curious.'

'And so am I.'

'About what?'

'About why a man like you would come here to work with us. A man with but one name and the look of someone who is no stranger to trouble comes to work with a Mexican crew and for one of the most evil men anywhere. Perhaps if you were to tell me the real reason you are here I could in turn tell you why I stay on.'

'I'd like to do that, Sanchez, but I don't figure I can.'

The foreman nodded, as this was the answer he'd anticipated.

'Then it would seem we both have our secret reasons for working on the place I always think of as Rancho Antiguo, *hombre*.'

'Reckon we do at that.' Vallery's look was searching. 'I just hope that our reasons don't one day bring us up against one another.'

'Perhaps I feel the same. But, then, you are *Americano*, I am Mexican . . .' Sanchez let the sentence hang unfinished. He shrugged as though the difference in nationality might in itself prove enough to cause conflict.

'Men like Braden are hard to beat,' Vallery declared after a silence.

'I do not know what you mean.'

'Maybe you don't. But I still feel I've got to point it out. Such men are winners, Sanchez. They aren't like everyday folks. They set their sights on something and they take it. They never quit easy.'

79

'You speak like a man who has perhaps been defeated by Rand Braden himself.'

It was a disturbing observation for the man to make. But Dev let it ride. He shrugged.

'All I know is that I wouldn't care to buck him,' he said with an air of finality.

'There are many different kinds of strength. Braden's strength is money. With money, he has won power, land and even a beautiful wife.'

'What do you mean . . . about the wife?'

'You have met the *señora*. Do you not think it strange that a woman of her beauty, whom any *hombre* might worship, would, of all her suitors, choose one such as Braden.'

'You just listed his assets . . .'

'Perhaps I should not speak openly before you, as anything I say may well be carried back to Braden. Yet I do not really fear the man. So I will tell you straight that the man bought his wife for solid cash. I shall not give you details, other than to say that Evalina's life was such that you could not possibly imagine. She found herself alone and in danger, and Braden was there with his offer and the *dinero* to back it up. He paid a powerful man ten thousand American dollars cash, and Evalina was his. An *hombre* who saw it all has made this public below the border.'

'And who would that be?'

Sanchez looked proud. 'None other than Carrado himself.'

Vallery frowned. 'The name rings a bell . . . Oh yeah. Is that the *bandido* they call the gringo-fighter or some such fanciful name?'

80

'He was there. And Carrado does not lie.'

'I can't believe all this.'

'Believe it or not, that is no concern of mine.' Sanchez kicked his horse. 'Come, it grows dark.'

Vallery sat his saddle staring after the man for long moments before heeling after him. He didn't catch up but rode at a leisurely trot savoring a freshly lighted durham. Eventually the cigarette went out but he didn't seem to notice. The rangeland was being swallowed by the night and the first stars winked out, but he didn't seem to notice them either. All he was seeing was the dazzling elfin face of Evalina Braden framed by raven hair, the latent wildness in her jade green eyes subdued in the last glance she had given him the night of the supper, almost as though pleading with him.

But for what?

He shook the image away and closed on Sanchez, who seemed locked in his own thoughts as the homestead lights loomed through the cedars. He didn't believe it. Sanchez hated Braden, would say anything to discredit the man.

Yet he found that the seed of unease, once sown, was hard to shake. Hadn't America gone to war over the evil of slavery?

'You make lousy coffee, Sheriff,' Joe Nells remarked, setting his battered and chipped enamel mug down on Kirby's spur-scarred desktop.

'That's about the only crime I'd willingly admit to, Marshal,' Muleshoe's peace officer conceded almost sadly. He tapped the brown bottle at his elbow. 'But I warned you she needed priming. Want to try it with a shot of rye? Even my joe starts to taste like milk and honey after about three mugs.'

'I don't drink while working, Sheriff.'

'Me neither,' Brown assured even as he deliberately poured a generous splash of whiskey to his coffee, then stirred it vigorously with a pencil. 'Now, what brings you to Muleshoe?'

Nells took out a brier pipe and began filling it from a worn tobacco-pouch. The marshal was a grey man whom no sun could redden for long. His eyes were agate-grey and his hair dust-grey and tonight he wore a worn shirt that was covered with the grey dust of long travel. He was a man of dignity with a spare, hard body, who had a way of speaking that made people listen. His hands, corded with veins and callused, were sure and strong and there was an economy in everything he did.

As a manhunter, he had a reputation for doggedness and success earned over many years.

'I'm searching for a fugitive from Flint River, Sheriff,' he supplied when he had the brier going to his satisfaction. He removed the pipe from between his teeth and jabbed it at the array of Wanted dodgers ornamenting the wall above the gunracks. 'That one with the beard. Vallery.'

Brown squinted up at the flyer. After a time he shook his head and grunted.

'Sorry, Marshal. We get all kinds coming through here, but I know I ain't sighted that one. Kinda impressive for a badman, ain't he? Not the kind of mug a man'd readily forget.'

'Well, I only came by on the offchance anyway.' The marshal sounded weary. 'Lost his trail weeks back in the Antelope mountains.'

Brown studied the dodger again. 'Don't really have the killer look about him though, does he?'

'Some of them don't.'

'Guess that's so.' Brown sipped his laced brew. For a man who professed abstinence on duty, he boasted a fine whiskey complexion. 'You look beat, Marshal. You want to doss here tonight?' The sheriff knew the marshal's salary wouldn't run to fancy fixings while on the trails.

'I just might do that. But mebbe I'll look around some more first – might make my way down to Hobo Town . . .'

'Just a moment.'

'What is it, Sheriff?'

Brown was on his feet studying the dodgers intently. He turned sharply.

'Just recalled something,' he said with a hint of excitement. 'The old memory ain't as rusty as I thought.'

'Does it concern Vallery?'

'Kind of . . . I guess. Mighty curious it was, Marshal. But one night, quite a spell back now but I remember it clear now; I was fast asleep when this feller came banging on my door around midnight. Big rich feller by the name of Braden, as I recall. You've heard of him, of course.'

'Everybody has. What did he want?'

'He was asking about some feller he thought might be wanted. Never gave no explanation, but asked me to turn out my dodgers . . . got a drawer stuffed with them over there. When he came to one on your man he asked me if he could take it, in case he should run into the feller, so I let him have it and he skee-daddled.'

Marshal Joe Nells wasn't looking weary any longer as he leaned across the desk.

'And that's it? Nothing else?'

'Nothing. I never saw Braden around after, so I reckon he must've just left town. What do you make of it, Marshal?'

Nells wasn't sure. Analysing what he'd been told, it didn't seem like too much. But after fruitless weeks on the trail he supposed maybe he was ready to grab at straws.

'How far is Buffalo Gate Ranch from here do you calculate, Sheriff?' he asked at length.

'Two – three days' ride. You figuring on following Braden up, Marshal?'

Nells looked up at the dodger. Gold-bearded Vallery had made both the prisons department and the law look bad when he broke jail and made good his escape. Nells took that sort of thing personally.

'I guess I am, Brown.' He glanced at the cells. 'Could you call me at first light?'

'Sure thing. Feel like a nightcap now?'

'I believe I do, Sheriff. Now.'

The marshal retired in what was, for this aging manhunter, a good mood. But it couldn't last, and didn't. He was preparing for the long journey south when the wire arrived from headquarters. An emergency. He was to return immediately. Why was it, he thought bitterly, that luck always appeared to favor ones who least deserved it?

Vallery eased his body gratefully into the big wooden tub and lay motionless, letting the warm water do its soothing work on saddle-aching limbs. He gave himself a solid five minutes' soaking, then set about working up a good lather with a fragrant slab of lemon-scented soap.

It was Saturday night and quiet on Buffalo Gate. After a back-busting week, the round-up had been completed just that day and the herd was secure in the marshalling yards out at Two Mile Sink.

Every available man was posted at the sink, with the exception of the house staff and the newest member of the work force. They were standing guard over the stock and making preparations for the drive to Fort James scheduled for tomorrow or the following day, depending on the weather.

Many of the hands had complained that it would be impossible to complete the round-up in the assigned time. But Braden had given them until the Saturday and he'd got what he wanted, as always.

Despite pressure and harsh conditions, Vallery had been enjoying the work when Braden sent Yancey out at around five to tell him he was required at the house. It turned out Braden had only wanted to discuss details of the upcoming drive, something that occupied only half an hour, and Dev had been dismissed when Braden's banker had arrived from town.

Suited him.

Now, clean, relaxed and refreshed, he climbed out of the tub, dried off leisurely and donned fresh gear. By the light of the lantern he combed his hair, using a cracked slab of mirror hung on the wall, then trimmed his beard with scissors.

He paused to study his sun-bronzed image in the glass. He'd lost weight through the work but knew he looked far better than he had at Muleshoe. The hunted look appeared to be gone. Flint River seemed a long way in the past.

He strapped on his gunbelt and stepped into the yard, where he stood savoring the evening coolness. Up the slope, the lights of the great house glowed warmly, and the banker's sulky was still standing out front. The clattering coming from the cookshack announced that Benito had recovered from his 'accident' sufficiently to supervise supply preparations for the drive.

He grinned.

Ever since the shoot-out, Benito had been his best friend, going out of his way to see that Vallery got the best cuts and his pick of the sweets. The rest of the crew still didn't seem to trust him, but they treated him with respect, which was all he wanted.

After a time he started off slowly on a long circuit around the headquarters and orchard. He was aware that Braden liked to take this walk; it made the man feel secure to relax now and again and appreciate his possessions. Dev sensed that the big man now almost trusted him, which he supposed made him one of a chosen three – himself, Mrs Latimer and Yancey.

He was not sure that the biggest man in the county

completely trusted his beautiful wife. He sure as hell didn't trust his crew.

Dev massaged the back of his neck as he walked around the breaking-yards and on towards the orchards.

His feelings towards Evalina Braden were mixed. He considered her quite stunning, was stimulated by her vivacity and high spirits, yet never forgot what he'd been told about the conditions surrounding her marriage.

He supposed it was simple coincidence that he seemed to run into her most every day.

Braden would invite him in for a whiskey, she would be there. One day he encountered her riding the range alone and rode all the way back to the house with her as escort, getting a calling down from Sanchez for neglecting his duties in the process.

Mornings it seemed she was always out on the balcony of her bedroom when he rode out.

A vain man might imagine the woman was interested in him. He didn't. But it did seem Evalina Braden drew something from his company and that pleased him. Occasionally she asked questions concerning his past but that was a closed book. One night, strolling as he was now, he'd heard sounds of argument from the rear of the house, her voice and Braden's raised in anger. He thought he heard a slap. He'd stopped and watched a while, felt a chill of unease as Yancey appeared in that spooky way he had, some distance away, to stand staring at the lights and cracking his knuckles.

The giant's official designation here was as Mrs

Braden's personal bodyguard. Why did she need one, unless it was against her husband?

He cut his thoughts off there.

When you were a man with a life-sentence hanging over your head, who'd come to a place such as this seeking seclusion and anonymity, you did your level best to keep your mouth shut, stay out of trouble and not pay too much attention to things going on around you that you might not care for.

Maybe Evalina Braden had troubles; he simply couldn't see how they could be as serious as his own, or was there a touch of self-pity in that?

The night wind had shifted by the time he arrived at the south-west corner of the orchard to fashion a quirly. From here he could see the lights of the Mexicans' village a mile across the flats. The married hands had sought permission for wives and families to move into the headquarters outbuilding for protection while the menfolk were posted out at the sink. Braden had refused. He continued to treat the workers badly. Sanchez insisted Braden was punishing the entire crew because a couple of *vaqueros* had lost some thirty head in a cliff stampede three days earlier. Dev had been there when the rancher denied their request. He'd seemed to enjoy it. He was as hard a man as he'd ever met, this good Samaritan who'd given him sanctuary.

Moving on, he found he couldn't help wondering if Braden mightn't be making a major mistake in coming down so hard on his workers at this particular time. His reasoning was simple.

He knew workers always grouched, and maybe

Buffalo Gate hands did so more than most. But in recent days he'd sensed a shift in mood amongst the *vaqueros* and it sure wasn't a change for the good.

Men talking intensely broke off at his approach. They gathered in serious groups during work-breaks and there was no laughter or joshing as there had been before. Occasionally he overheard Braden's name mentioned, and once when the big man had taken a tumble from his horse he'd heard a young rider hiss: 'Tromp him, horse, and we make you a hero!'

Everyday stuff?

Maybe so. Yet Vallery didn't think so. He'd been aware from the outset that Braden was hated here but it seemed that something stronger than that was in the air now.

The moon was up and the south-western stars filled the sky as he began making his way back to the house. Lost in thought, he was looking away from the ornamental trees to his left when he heard a stir of movement.

He dropped hand to gunbutt and whirled in a crouch.

'Who's there? Show yourself!'

He heard a startled sound then glimpsed a slender figure in the shadows. 'Dev? Is that you?'

It was Evalina's voice. He would know it anywhere.

'Why are you out here?' he asked gruffly. 'You shouldn't wander away from the house at night.'

'I have nothing to fear here, Dev,' she said quietly.

He had to concede this was very likely true. To a man, the Mexicans whose feelings for Braden spanned the spectrum from dislike and envy to burning hatred, seemed to treat the big man's young wife almost with a kind of reverence. She was beautiful, sure, but there seemed to be more to their affection than that.

Just another minor mystery in the day-to-day life on Buffalo Gate Ranch? Most likely, he thought soberly.

They were relatively safe here in the hay barn, he supposed. Even so, he kept one eye on a chink in the wall-planking that enabled him to overlook most of the lamplit yard.

'The banker left yet?' he asked.

'Not yet. They were talking business when I left the house.'

Vallery nodded and continued gazing toward the house. The woman watched him closely for a time, then asked curiously:

'What is it, Dev?'

'Guess I'm looking for your shadow. Seems I don't often sight you without him lurking in the background somewhere.'

'I tricked him and slipped away. I shouldn't do that, I know, but he doesn't ever get angry with me. Poor Yancey . . .'

'Why do you say that?'

'I don't believe he really wants to spend his whole life tagging after me. But he's terrified some harm might come to me.'

'He must have his reasons for feeling that way.'

She glanced away. 'Oh, he does, he certainly does.'

'Do you want to explain what you mean by that?'

He thought he sounded like a stern schoolteacher. The truth of it was, all the undercurrents, secrecy, odd behaviour and tension was beginning to make him edgy. And he wasn't too relaxed about standing here in a barn at night with the boss man's wife, and her weird protector maybe mooching about someplace, watching him.

She gave him a strange look.

'Things are seldom as they seem, Just Dev.' She called him that sometimes for some reasons of her own, yet didn't really seem to find it at all unusual that this appeared to be all the name he had.

'Braden never seems to worry about your safety. Why should Yancey?'

'My husband knows nobody will harm me as the situation is.' She pouted prettily. 'Anyway, why are we wasting good gossiping time discussing that? Tell me, Dev, what's the latest from the round-up? Who's plotting to harm my husband next?'

He shook his head slowly.

'This kind of talk doesn't sit well with me, Evalina.' He didn't know whom he could trust on Buffalo Gate, so trusted or confided in nobody.

'You don't have to be annoyed. I know what goes on. But if it upsets you, then we'll let it go. After all, I'm just a silly woman and not to be taken too seriously, aren't I.' She slipped an arm through his. 'Walk me to the house, my very serious Just Dev?'

The short stroll proved uneventful, with Vallery stiff and watchful, the woman swinging off his arm like a young girl on her way to the big dance with her first beau.

Watching her dance up the steps as lightly as a dancer, he wondered what it would be like to have such a vivid beauty as your wife. Much the same as it must be to own all the land you could see and be a law unto yourself, he supposed.

He thought that sounded envious, which wasn't really the way he felt tonight. The longer the round-up continued and with each uneventful week sliding by into the past, he was loosing his edginess, feeling safer by the day. And he had barely felt anything like safe since the day he left the law cursing in his dust.

Standing in the wide yard by a light-pole, he heard the sound of wheels crunching gravel coming from the far side of the hacienda. Moments later the banker's stylish brougham was to be seen wheeling away through the title gate, the stiff-necked little money-grubber sitting bolt upright as he plied the ribbons, probably stiff as a plank from Braden's imported port.

He turned and glanced back at the gallery where he glimpsed a shape blotting out half a lighted window at the servants' quarters. He threw Yancey a big salute but received no response. As he crossed the yard he realized he was still wide awake despite the hour and with the prospect of another long day in the saddle tomorrow.

He went to the stables, to be greeted by his good horse. The animal needed grooming, and he'd been at it for several minutes by the dim light of a low-turned lantern, when he heard the sound of hoof-beats.

Brush in hand, he went to the window and peered

out. Two riders were coming in under the high-arched gateway, swinging towards the front of the hacienda. He immediately recognized the Mexican hand in charro pants and enormous sombrero as Rodriguez, the sentry from the main gate. There appeared to be something familiar about the second man, but it wasn't until he drew abreast of the livery, with the yard lights falling across both riders, that recognition struck like a club.

The dusty horseman astride the trail-stained mare was Marshal Joe Nells.

CHAPTER 7

THE THREAT

It took a lot to intimidate Braden's housekeeper. A stern and forbidding woman in her mid-fifties, Mrs Latimer had been the first Mrs Braden's personal servant. Following the death of Evalina's predecessor, she'd consented to remain on as head of the household staff at Braden's insistence. The only person the woman ever deferred to was the cattle king himself.

'You will kindly knock the dust from your clothing before you enter, if you please, sir,' she announced, standing skinny and stiff-backed in her severe black dress in the doorway.

Nells obliged. She stared significantly at his boots. He wiped them on the backs of his trouser-legs. Mrs Latimer sniffed and turned away.

'Follow me, sir.'

She guided the lawman to the door of Braden's study, motioned for him to wait, vanished inside.

'A Marshal Nells, Mr Braden,' she announced.

'Shall I show him in?'

Braden shot a sharp glance across at Yancey.

'It's all right,' he said reassuringly. 'Your slate is clean.' He nodded to the woman. 'I'll see him.'

Nells entered holding his hat at his side. Braden rose from his desk to shake hands and went to the sideboard to pour drinks.

'What can I do for you, Marshal?'

Nells didn't answer immediately. He was staring hard at the giant humpback. Yancey met his stare, eyes expressionless.

'Don't I know your face from someplace, mister?' the lawman demanded.

'My personal bodyguard and trusted servant, Yancey,' Braden supplied smoothly, handing Nells his glass. 'Former Rio outlaw, now reformed. Doubtless you are recalling him from some ancient Wanted dodger, Marshal. But you can take my word for it that there is nothing against his name now. Your very good health.' Nells accepted his glass but didn't drink.

'Yancey, Yancey . . .' he murmured, sucking the ends of his tattered mustache. When it came to criminals, the man had the memory of an elephant. Suddenly he snapped his fingers and put a sharper stare on the impassive man against the wall. 'Rio! That gave me the clue. You were an associate of that so-called rebel, Carrado. Right?'

'Right,' sighed Braden. 'Carrado it was, but—'

'Carrado, the man responsible for the uprising of Sabinosa! Correct?' His tone was scornful, contemptuous. 'The gringo-fighter, the *paisanos*' champion?

95

That Carrado?' For a moment Rand Braden's powerful features seemed pale, dark eyes glittering cold. The name 'Carrado' was never spoken in this house or on his ranch. There were reasons for this that Nells would know nothing about, but they had to do with a dramatic series of events in Chihuahua several years earlier in which a rebel leader had been captured at a ranch named Palo Pinto, and the rebel's woman had found herself a wealthy gringo 'protector' by the name of Braden.

'That Carrado,' Braden said grimly. Then he brightened. 'Now serving a life term in some jungle hell-hole prison in Chihuahua, or by now most likely dead.'

He paused, straightened and walked briskly to a wall cabinet, opened it. 'But before you get carried away, take a look at this, Nells.'

The document folder he produced bore the official seal of Mexico in one corner. He passed it to the lawman in silence. Nells scanned it briskly but thoroughly. It stated quite unequivocally that an agreement had been made upon the capture of the notorious Carrado that his bodyguard was considered simple-minded and therefore was not to be held accountable for Carrado's crimes. It concluded that the *alcalde* of Otago Province had personally agreed to the man's being released into the custody of one Rand Braden, at Braden's request.

'Harrumph!' sneered Nells. 'South of the border law enforcement!' With a last stare at Yancey he gulped down half his drink and concentrated on his host. 'In any case, I'm here on a very different matter, Mr Braden. Looking for a man. A condemned killer and escapee by the name of Devereaux Vallery. Do you perchance know anything of this desperado?'

'Not a damn thing, Marshal. Why? Should I?'

'Muleshoe law office, sir. That ring a bell?'

'Not readily,' Braden replied, perching on the edge of his desk and swinging his leg leisurely.

'Look, mister, I happen to know that you—'

'Oh, *that* Vallery!' Braden said snapping his fingers. 'Of course. Afraid I quite forgot that trifling incident—'

'The incident when you appeared at the law office, examined a Wanted dodger on this man Vallery, then left with a copy in great haste,' Nells finished for him. 'And vanished from Muleshoe next morning. You can explain, of course.'

'Of course. As you were doubtless informed, I'd visited the jailhouse on another matter earlier that day and saw all those posters on the walls. Later I saw this fellow who I thought resembled one of those felons, so I went and got a copy of the poster, as your sheriff declares.' He grinned broadly and spread his hands wide. 'Nothing like him. Chalk and cheese. Now, Marshal, is there anything else I can help you with?'

Nells appeared to deflate. The Vallery case was becoming something of an obsession. He was neglecting other duties to concentrate on the killer-escaper. Braden was nothing if not convincing, but the marshal was a hard man to deter.

'Appreciate your time, Mr Braden. I reckon you

won't object if I ask to be put up overnight? Stables will do me fine.'

'What on earth for, man?'

Before Nells could answer Evalina strolled grace-fully into the lamplit room, a wide-eyed innocent with the walk of a famished cat.

The marshal stared. A bunch of armed *vaqueros* in the yard and the presence of the hulking bodyguard, along with Braden's arrogance, had unsettled him. But the stunning young woman left him scratching his head. He knew the range country and some of the great houses well, but this hacienda certainly seemed full of surprises.

'Aren't you going to introduce me to your guest, darling?' Evalina smiled.

'No, I'm not.' Braden's face was stone. He turned to Nells. 'Sorry, it's not convenient to put you up, sir. Now or at any other time. You may excuse yourself if you wish.'

'Very well, sir,' Nells said stiffly, collecting his hat. He shrugged. 'I suppose it was a pretty flimsy lead at that.'

'Does this mean you will have to give up on this man, Vallery?' Braden asked coolly, walking him to the door.

'For the time being, yes.'

'Too bad. If there's anything I detest it's an evil-doer getting away with his crimes.'

'Oh, he won't get away. We get them all, sooner or later.' Nells nodded. 'Thanks for your time, sir.'

'Any time, Marshal, any time. Yancey, show the marshal out, will you?'

The two quit the room and Braden returned to the decanter to pour another drink. He stared at his wife but didn't speak. Soon they heard the horse move off outside, and presently Yancey filled the doorway.

Braden didn't turn his head as he said: 'Go find him and bring him here.'

'Dev?' Yancey grunted.

'Of course Dev, you fool.'

'He's not a fool,' Evalina defended as the giant walked out.

Braden swung to face his wife, now seated upon a high stool with the drink she'd poured for herself.

'He is a fool, and you know better than involve yourself in my business matters, Mrs Braden. Now, get out!'

Defiance flared momentarily in the woman's eyes but she drained her glass and quit the room without reply. Yancey watched her go before turning and leaving. Braden smiled and lifted the glass to his lips.

'Another, Dev?'

Vallery stared at his empty glass, then passed it to Braden.

'I reckon I could use another after what you just told me.'

'I'm sure you can. But I wouldn't be too concerned. That hangdog lawman was obviously intimidated by me and the way I treated him, like a menial nobody. Everybody can be bluffed, and lawmen are no exception. I walked all over the man. At the end he almost thanked me for refusing to put him up overnight. They know when they are out of their depth. I doubt we'll be hearing any more from Marshal Nells.'

Vallery accepted his glass with a frown.

'You took one hell of a risk lying to him bare-faced that way.'

'Yes, I did, didn't I?'

'Why?'

'Simple. You're far more valuable to me here than breaking rocks in Yuma for the rest of your life. I'm happy to say that the potential I recognized in you at Muleshoe has proven even greater than I expected.' He gestured at the windows. 'The hands realized fast that you're my man and can't be bluffed. That's more important to me than you know, right now . . . although I still don't trust the bastards . . .'

He paused for a moment with a scowl, then brightened as he held his glass up to the light. 'And of course now I feel I can rely upon you even more than before.'

'How do you figure that?'

'Isn't it obvious? You see, we are very much alike, Dev. We both believe in paying our dues, good or bad. You were in my debt before, now you are totally so.'

Dev didn't like that. He rose and set down his full glass.

'You're wrong about that, Braden,' he said bluntly. 'I'm quitting.'

'What the hell do you mean?'

'I reckon I've covered what I owe, including what you just did for me with Nells.'

Braden stared at him intensely.

'You sound anything but convincing, loser. What's the real reason behind this extraordinary statement? Come on, the least you owe me is the truth.'

Dev sucked in a big breath, held it in, slowly exhaled. Trouble was, the other was right. He did owe. He owed big time, and he always paid his debts. But his decision to quit had been prompted by Nells' sudden appearance. He'd considered himself safe here on the Buffalo Gate, but now that feeling had been shattered. Sure he owed Braden. But owed it to himself to stay alive and out of Yuma one hell of a lot more.

There was another reason as well.

During his time here he'd witnessed the true harshness of the Mexicans' lives, their semi-poverty and humiliation. He was no bleeding heart but was a man of feelings, whereas the powerful figure studying him intently now appeared to have none.

And last but not least, was the inexplicable. He'd had an uneasy feeling about Buffalo Gate since his first day. There seemed to exist in the very air itself here a strange sense of foreboding, an undercurrent of uncertainty that simply couldn't be denied. He was aware of such matters as the fact that Braden beat his young wife, that every Mexican over two years of age hated him, that the boss man rode everyone harder and harder with each passing day.

Something had to bust here eventually, maybe even explode. He was sure of it, could feel it in his bones. And one thing was for sure. An escaped criminal with $1,000 on his head had no business being around when the big bang came and Buffalo Gate was crawling with law as a result.

But he had to be fair and felt he was obliged to inform Braden of his concerns before leaving.

The rancher just laughed.

'You've been listening to all the hate they spew out, the big plans they've got to do me in, the whole comedy. And that's all it is. A huge joke.'

'I don't think so. There's been a change in the air lately. I've felt it, tasted it. Trouble's brewing, believe me.'

'Well, what if what you are saying was proven true. Do you mean you'd still quit, just when I needed a loyal, strong man at my side most?'

'I reckon.'

Braden stepped back. 'Fine, go ahead. Who knows? You might even get as far as off my acres by the time Marshal Nells hears that we've been harboring his killer here, although I doubt it.'

Dev's eyes flared.

'You'd turn me in?'

'Mister, I'd turn my own momma in if she—'

That was as far as he got. Emotion suddenly got the better of Dev. He was an innocent man living the life of a fugitive, and in that moment a threatening Braden seemed to represent all the blind power and injustice of the forces ranged against him.

His swing was lightning-fast but Braden was faster. Bobbing low, he came up slugging, his first punch crunching Vallery's jaw, the second skimming off his brow as he swayed out of reach.

They clinched fiercely, with knees, elbows, fists

and headbutts doing quick damage before Vallery found himself being borne backwards.

He stared down. A huge hand imprisoned his right shoulder and he twisted to stare up into the impassive face of Yancey. He exerted every ounce of his strength to break free but he was locked tight, his whole shoulder beginning to go numb.

'Once a loser, always a loser, Vallery.'

Braden was breathing hard and leaking blood from a mouth gash as he stood before him, swaying slightly on his feet. He spat on the floor, sleeved his lips, grinned.

'All right, you can leave him go, Yancey,' he ordered, and the hand dropped instantly, leaving Vallery with a half-frozen right arm. Contemptuously then, Braden turned his back on him and hefted his drink. 'Feel better with that out of your system, Dev? Sure you do. And think about it. You don't really want to leave here. You've got it made. You've shown you can do what I hired you for, you're on top of the greasers, my wife thinks you're good-looking and we're ahead on the round-up. Ride off my land and you're back to what you were at Muleshoe – a nothing on the run with no more future than a snowball in hell.'

He snapped his fingers and gestured expansively. He was enjoying this. 'You certainly haven't always made the smart decisions in your loser life, Dev, but show you can change. Why in hell would a man in your position want to leave?'

Why indeed?

Subdued, hurting, forcing himself to look at

things clearly, Vallery had to ask himself that question. What if trouble was brewing on Buffalo Gate? Surely he could handle it? And if he worried about the changing mood of the crew, hadn't he handled tougher problems than that before?

What was the alternative? Run like a dog and likely die like one?

'You've got a way of getting your point across, Braden.'

'Does that mean you'll stay?'

'Yeah.'

The gringo-fighter swore softly, yet with a forgiving smile.

His stolen burro was willing enough to try and carry its rider through some of the roughest terrain in the Chihuahua high country, but it simply wasn't designed for the task. Its legs were too short, it was long past its prime years and showed it with every step as it snorted laboriously up the inclines and wheezed asthmatically going down the far side.

The rider was patient, even though anything but a patient man. With long legs wrapped round the sorry animal's barrel and a battered sombrero tilted back from a recklessly handsome face, he alternately whistled an old Andalusian love-song or simply leaned back, hung on to the belly-rope and reflected upon his recent good fortune.

He might not look a lucky man at the moment but looks could be deceiving.

On the negative side he might indeed be hungry, hunted, saddle-sore and trying desperately to worm his way through the Federalista country of Otago Province, all alone and almost out of ammo. On the other hand, he was still alive while the brave *compañeros* who'd set out with him on this journey from the southern hell-hole prison were all dead.

Just three days earlier the exuberant *paisano*, whom the poor called a hero and whom the rich wished exterminated, had been leaving behind the last of the jungle country which, one by one, had claimed his brave *compañeros*. The authorities boasted that Ojo jail did not really need guards to watch over its doomed inmates, that escapers never survived the disease-ridden jungle with its wild beasts and venomous reptiles.

The day Carrado actually decided to put that theory to the test was the day he got the brutal head guard with a home-made knife, and the so-called Otago Four went over the wall, to take their chances.

Manuel and Teofilo were sick with the fevers within twenty-four hours, so much so that when they attempted to swim the first major river, Manuel was swept away. The following day Teofilo was bitten by a poisonous snake and died in great agony.

Diego survived until they met the jaguar.

Gabriel Carrado was a brave one, yet he'd felt terror constrict his bowels as never before the moment they looked up from the lizard they were attempting to cook for supper, to stare into the fathomless yellow eyes gazing unblinking at them from steaming green undergrowth, a bare few feet distant.

Almost as lithe and supple as a jungle cat himself, Carrado somersaulted backwards into deep brush, leaving the brave Diego ice-locked in terror as the beast emitted a roar like the wrath of God and struck. He counted himself lucky that dear Diego had been the only plump inmate in the prison, otherwise the spotted terror might have finished with him quickly and come after him.

Twenty-four hours later saw him reach a point in a high trail in the cattle country from where he could see the white-painted horse-yards and yellow-tiled rooftops of the Palo Pinto Ranch of Emil Conrade.

Memory went clicking back, vivid, painful. . . .

The rebel rarely made mistakes.

A man who dared ally himself with the cause of the countless poor against the bloated land-barons and corrupt law of the *ricos* in sad Chihuahua, and set himself up as some kind of leader in the struggle, might be allowed perhaps one major mistake.

That day, after weeks in the mountains evading the Third Otago Rurales, Carrado, his bodyguard and his beautiful woman made their mistake. Coming to the Palo Pinto Ranch country just on dusk and weary to the bone, they rode directly to the ranch house with the intention of holding it up and taking desperately needed food and arms.

How were they to know that the gringo *ranchero*, Conrade, was playing host to one of the most powerful ranchers from across the border: Rand Braden.

Braden had arrived with a dozen heavily armed men who got the drop on Carrado's party before they were even aware of them.

Carrado was philosophical. Capture or death were

everlastingly nipping at his heels. But while waiting for the Rurales to arrive, he realized that capture and possibly death were not the worst things that could befall a reckless *paisano.*

He'd expected his woman would go to prison with him – until Braden, obviously entranced – offered Conrade the rancher a large sum in American dollars if he would hand Evalina over to him and inform the authorities she had escaped.

In his frenzied rage, the best the rebel could negotiate was for Conrade also to release Yancey in order that the giant simpleton could accompany the Buffalo Gate party north as protector of Braden's 'bride to be'.

Still he could scarcely believe that this worst experience of his life could have taken place as it had done, with two rich men deciding the fate of a human being as though she were no better than an animal.

He came out of his bitter reverie, and blinked.

Had he been less weary, hungry and desperate to reach the Rio Grande, Carrado might have been tempted to make his way down there, wait until nightfall, then creep into that fine house and split Emil Conrade from crotch to Christmas with his good blade.

But just thinking of her and how many hard miles, high risks and ugly people with guns lay between this spot where he stood and his destination, made him settle for a mocking salute for the *ranchero* who'd seen him off to Ojo, then kick on north.

Eventually the narrow twisting trail led him to the

flank of the red bluff which seemed almost to hang over the Shadrack, a long, long way down, a shining, sparkling stream that gurgled across white stones in its shallow bed.

The rider licked his lips as he stared ahead. The Shadrack was the last of the many creeks he'd had to cross since putting the rangelands behind him. Beyond its tree-lined banks lay nothing but rough country leading all the way to the Rio and America – end of the line.

The journey down was a penance. He didn't whistle or sing any more and after an hour was forced to dismount and let the burro follow him down the best way it might.

And so he reached the Shadrack.

There he hunkered down in trailside brush for a full hour, as motionless as a stone, the big old-fashioned revolver in his fist, a man of the outdoors with the patience of a saint.

He kept sniffing as if he could smell Federales.

There was a stronghold several miles westward beyond this only fording in miles of high bluffs, and the hated Sonoran provincial police liked to boast that the only outlaws they allowed to cross the river, whether travelling north or south, did so in coffins.

He grinned. Some joke.

Eventually, as the shadows grew long upon the land, he took the burro's rope and let it into the water. The animal balked and he turned to locate it. The flat, whiplike crack of a rifle sounded loud and clear above the rushing of the stream. The man felt the airwhip of its passage as it passed beneath his unshaven jaw, then slammed into the burro's skull, killing it where it stood.

He dived under.

With slugs peppering the water like hail, he let the current carry him downstream until his lungs howled for mercy. He came up within a nest of lichened grey boulders and kicked ashore as the afternoon filled with shouting and gunshots – all upstream.

He grinned like a wolf as he vanished in the woods. They thought they'd killed him.

Suddenly it was peaceful again. The stream burbled on, the clear waters stained pink with the burro's blood. From the low fork of a tree, he watched and waited with the old pistol in his hand. Whether it would fire after being submerged was something he'd find out when the time came. There was no thought of flight. He was half-starved, twenty miles from the Rio, afoot in Federale country and enraged. Mostly he was enraged, and that mostly boded ill for someone. There was neither sight nor sound of the ambushers or their horses. But he hadn't heard them go, which meant they were still here, either celebrating his death or lying in wait for him to show himself.

He dropped belly-flat and wriggled through brush and stones for a quarter-mile until he was in a nest of boulders beyond the bend in the stream where the attack had been launched.

Nothing stirred.

He lay as still as death, waiting.

There was a sudden flare of light not a hundred feet distant where two logs had been tossed ashore by some flood. A hand cupped a match to a cigarette and for a long moment the hatchet face of the grey-garbed Federale was briefly illuminated by a soft, yellow glow.

He raised the revolver and triggered.

Everything happened at once. The smoker dropped like a stone and a long lance of gunflame reached towards Carrado's position from the fork of a tree where the rifleman had been waiting.

Carrado rolled and fanned gun-hammer, the river-side rocking to the angry argument of guns that rose to a crescendo until a dark shape plummeted from the tree and nose-dived into the earth.

Silence.

He had one bullet left but didn't have to use it. After waiting a full half-hour without moving and barely breathing, he rose confidently and went forward.

As he'd figured, there were just two of them. He plundered their pockets for money and tobacco, helped himself to a fob-watch with a handsome inscription and went searching for their mounts.

It was dusk two nights later when a man and two tired horses swam the fabled Rio, and Carrado the rebel set foot on American soil for the first time in three brutal years.

CHAPTER 8

THE BREATH
OF HATE

The hot, resinous smells of early summer hung heavy in the air of Buffalo Gate that night as Oteros, Balthazar and Benito visited the isolated adobe of Miguel Sanchez.

They found the ramrod seated on his stoop drinking coffee thick and black enough to stand unaided.

They brought bad news. Two days earlier Braden had broken the arm of Benito with a blow from a pick-handle when the hand accidentally added too much dip in the cattle trough, causing the death of three prime steers. The hands were enraged. They had waited long enough, they complained bitterly. When would Braden finally be dead and gone, leaving them free to press their claims for the *rancho* in the gringo courts? When?

They moved indoors where Sanchez stood with

brown hands resting on the table, staring broodingly into the flame of the candle. The feeble light threw his shadow hugely upon the baked-mud wall in back of him.

These were the most skilled hands on the ranch, as adept at wielding gun or blade as they were at roping a steer or applying a branding-iron.

There had been times during the days of the former *ranchero* when rustler bands from the south had plagued the then Rancho Antiguo, and Sanchez and his father had led the *vaqueros* against them. Sanchez had killed his first cow-thief with his bare hands, and there had been others after that. At the time the father died, and the gringo lawyers had done their evil work over law books and title deeds behind closed doors to deliver the *rancho* to Braden, Sanchez was an accomplished fighter and natural leader who, these days, often felt like neither.

Braden had bested him. Sanchez had schemed and plotted and half-drowned himself in tequila as he racked his brains in vain in search of the brilliant plan of action that might result in Braden's overthrow, followed by his accession to the throne of power at the hacienda.

His thoughts drifted back to the last time he'd tried to kill the rancher, several months before Dev came to the spread.

It was in the mountains. He'd had Braden lined up in his sights at easy range. He fired and had seen the bullet rip bark from a tree thirty feet from the powerful figure astride the black blood-horse.

Why had he missed so badly?

112

Fear.

He would admit it only to himself: that, from the first day Braden had ridden on to the land, he had typified for him all the ruthless power and authority of the gringos who were engulfing their lands. He was the invincible *Americano*. He'd sapped the owner's will to fight and had thrown him the bauble of ramrod, which he'd grabbed and clung to like a beggar.

Now, yet again, Braden had grossly mistreated a man, and his inner circle of 'plotters and rebels' – he could almost laugh at the meaningless names they gave themselves – wanted him to do something about it. Take action. Protest. Threaten to abandon the round-up if Braden didn't apologize and promise to mend his ways.

They left with nothing. Only Benito with his slinged arm seemed relieved.

Miguel Sanchez swapped coffee for tequila and went back outside under the big night sky. They considered him weak, he knew, but they were wrong. For some weeks now he had been aware of a change in himself and in many of the men. Others had noticed this phenomenon also, such as Dev. He'd told him so and asked what the cause might be.

Miguel said he didn't know, but this was a lie.

It was the whisper that was responsible, he knew. That word on the wind coming from the south, which had to do with a jailbreak, manhunts, death in the jungle and Federales in a rage.

And a name that sent a tingle through his wrists:

Carrado! The famed gringo-fighter and defender of all things Mexican!

He wouldn't know the *paisano* agitator from a peyote bush, but the man's name and recent history was as familiar to Buffalo Gate as their own.

Carrado was the freedom fighter who'd been captured on the Palo Pinto Ranch of Emil Conrade in Otago Province some years earlier, along with his woman. A deal of some kind had been struck down there after Carrado went to the jungle hell of Ojo Jail, the consequence of which had been Braden's returning from his visit to the ranch with his new young wife, formerly – or so it was rumored – the outlaw's lover.

It was a fascinating tale but the ramrod wasn't sure whether he fully believed it until it was revived recently with the rumor, or fiction, that Carrado had broken jail and was last heard of shooting his way north.

Sanchez wanted to believe it all, needed to believe. For right now, with the round-up going well and Dev keeping them in line on Braden's behalf, they appeared to be losing ground in their struggle.

What they needed was a saviour, someone to light the fire for them and maybe show them the way to regain what had been lost.

But maybe that was too much to expect of a man they didn't even know, who could simply be a figment of Mexican fiction for all they really knew.

He shook his head. No. He would not believe that.

He knew they had all waited too long. But now, daily, he was watching and waiting for the opportunity, the sign that it was time to strike.

He knew that when it came he and his brave *vaqueros* would be ready.

Smoke trickled from Vallery's lips as he stood leaning against a ghost-white tree gazing down on the ramrod's adobe.

He counted the four as they emerged and three crossed to their cayuses in the moonlight, Sanchez watching with arms folded from his rear stoop.

He did not know what had taken place down there but every instinct warned that it wasn't something that would benefit the Gate primarily, or Dev Vallery secondarily.

The three hands filling leather now were the ones he'd fallen into the habit of watching most closely, hence his vigilance here tonight.

They were the ones who talked most, were most likely to object to overwork or rough handling. And they, along with Sanchez, were the men in whom he'd most noticed the sudden change which seemed to be affecting the crew recently. They loped away and Sanchez disappeared inside.

Dev stroked his golden van Dyke beard thoughtfully.

Times like this he was forced to think hard on exactly who he was and what he was doing here. He had no liking or respect for Braden, yet their destinies were tied together. Braden treated him like a lackey, yet he had given him sanctuary and had recently shielded him from that old bloodhound, Nells.

A man had to be one thing or the other. And if he was beholden to Braden then he was obliged to look out for him.

Would he report what he'd seen here tonight? Should he tell the man he'd overheard the name 'Carrado' in whispered conversations at the yards? If he told the rancher he had some suspicions of certain men, how would Braden react?

His lips compressed. He knew the answer to that. Braden would react badly, he knew, and possibly innocent men could be hurt.

There was enough of that on Buffalo Gate without his contributing to it. So the best thing he could do for the moment was be silent but keep watchful.

He wondered if the *vaqueros* would thank him for his decision, were they aware of it. He smiled grimly and shook his head. Most likely not, he thought. The poor always felt stepped on, either by the bosses or the gods.

The knock on her door was discreet, yet firm.

'Mrs Braden?' the familiar voice called.

'What?'

'Mr Braden would like you to join him in the study.'

'Is the buyer still there?'

'Yes, Mrs Braden.'

'Then tell him I'll be by later . . . perhaps.'

The knob turned and the door opened to admit the housekeeper. Standing by the windows of her private quarters, Evalina whirled angrily, eyes flaring.

'Who gave you permission to come in? Get out!'

116

Mrs Latimer held her ground, a picture of correctness in starched linen and high collar.

'I'm sure you don't mean that, ma'am.'

'The hell I don't. *Apártate!* Tell my husband if he wants someone to pour drinks for that smelly cowdealer, there are any number of servants. Well, don't just stand there. Do as you are told!'

'As you wish, Mrs Braden.'

The door closed softly on the woman's rigid back. Evalina picked up a button-box and flung it at the door.

The tantrum made her feel better, although she knew her defiance wouldn't last. She would give in, she always did. Not from any feelings for the man she'd married but simply because whenever she defied him he made life so unpleasant that it was scarely worth it.

After a time she lighted a perfumed cigarette – which her husband hated – and strolled out on to her private balcony.

Familiar sounds came through the opened double-doors, the clatter of utensils from the scullery, the quick steps of maids up and down the corridors, the occasional sharp tones of Mrs Latimer.

If she dreamed at times like this of another life so impossibly different from this, no one could ever tell. Apart from the housekeeper, the staff women were very fond of her and loved to amuse themselves speculating on the half-truths of her past.

She drew deeply and flung the stub-end of her cigarette into the garden. Occasionally she heard her husband's voice coming from the study. He sounded angry with the dealer. An advance payment on his shipping herd, delivered at the railhead, had been made the previous day and was $2,000 less than he'd expected.

She didn't have to be in the study to picture the scene. The doors and windows would be wide open to catch the breeze and let the cigar-smoke escape. The buyer would probably be standing nervously, while from behind his desk Braden would berate him as he might the lowest hand on the spread.

In the end Braden would get his own way, no matter what the rights or wrongs. He always did.

She turned her head at a whisper of sound from the main corridor.

She glimpsed a shadow, then it was gone.

Yancey.

Evalina smiled. He was the only true friend she had in this still-alien place, a simple man who could bend a branding-iron with his bare hands. She was still amazed that they had allowed her to keep him with her that terrible day in Mexico when she was sold like a slave.

It seemed, even then, that Braden had realized that in the hostile environment of his ranch, where so many of his workers hated him, his new wife might become a target, hence the wisdom of a round-the-clock bodyguard.

Of course, Yancey had become Braden's lackey, held in check by Braden's threat to drum up some fake charge against him and have him shipped back to jail should he ever step out of line. One way or another, everyone here was his prisoner.

Even Dev.

'Dev,' she said aloud, and smiled.

It had been a good day when the blond-bearded horseman showed up on Buffalo Gate. They'd hit it off well and she found his presence reassuring. She liked to listen to him talk and the way he seemed to hold far distances in his eyes.

Time passed.

She was back in her room when she heard her husband's angry shout; 'Take him to the tack room and lock him in!'

She sighed. More trouble. She made her way to the kitchen where some maids stood listening by an open door.

'What?' she demanded. 'What is it this time?'

'Is trouble, *señora*,' said the cook. 'A thief has been caught.'

'A thief? Who?'

'Montoya,' a stern voice said from the scullery, and Mrs Latimer appeared. 'He was caught taking money from the housekeeping-box in the dining-room. I caught him red-handed and reported it to Mr Braden.'

'Pablo?' She couldn't believe it. Then she remembered the Montoyas' child was ill. The man had come to her a week ago for money to buy medicine. 'Did he say why he wanted the money?'

'Medicine.' The woman sniffed. 'What a pathetic lie.'

'It happens to be the truth,' Evalina flared, her eyes dangerous. 'Why didn't you come to me? I'd have given him the money. And why did you go running to my husband, as you always do?'

'And let a thief go unpunished.' The woman sniffed. 'To most of us here, thieving is a sin, ma'am. Most that is, not all.'

That was a thrust at her past, Evalina knew. She let it go and whirled away to go angrily down the corridor and out into the yard.

It took some time for her to cool down, and she was turning for the house with the intention of speaking to her husband on the matter when the mailrider clattered through the title gate.

'Ma'am,' he said. He tipped his hat and reached into his sack. 'Usual stuff for Mr Braden, a new Sears Roebuck catalogue and, oh yeah, one for you.'

She took the mail and stared at the envelope with her name on it. She never received any mail, didn't recognize the handwriting. It bore a Mexican postmark. She tore it open, unfolded the blank piece of white paper – and a dry red leaf floated to the ground.

Her hand flew to her breast. She bent and snatched up the leaf. In another life – a world as alien from the one she lived in now as the moon – she and the man she loved had employed such a signal when they needed to communicate anonymously and secretly.

She hadn't heard from Gabriel for three long years. Until now.

It was burning hot as the riders worked their way back towards headquarters. No breeze drifted down from the high mesas and no birds sang. All the cattle country lay panting under the harsh afternoon sun.

Vallery and Sanchez, with three Gate cowboys, came riding at a slow lope along the Greenwater Creek, shirts clinging to torsos with sweat, faces gleaming. They were searching for the new stud bull Braden had bought in last week and which had busted loose from its corral overnight. They had been hunting since breakfast, neglecting the round-up, and the $500 stud was still at large.

Sanchez held up his arm and they swung in beneath the shade of an ugly giant of a cottonwood on the creek bank.

'We shall rest five minutes,' the ramrod announced as he swung to ground.

Vallery got down in the shade to build a cigarette, eyes moving restlessly over the swales and gully-washes that marked the base of the mesa. He wore rough range gear and his face was darkly tanned, his beard bleached several shades lighter by the sun.

'Could be up there, Miguel,' he suggested when he had his smoke going.

'Maybe.'

'If you ask me he is gone, vamoosed,' opined a panting Oteros.

'Nobody is asking,' snapped Sanchez. The heat and the time-wasting search were putting them on edge.

Dev's eyes continued to play over the shimmering landscape. By this, he knew the Buffalo Gate as well as any *vaquero*. Over the long weeks it had become his world. He'd not left it since his arrival. At times he thought of the spread as his prison, at others as a refuge and place of sanctuary for a man with the baggage he was toting round.

He was watching the way heat waves caused the trees and boulders to seem to swim and ripple higher up the mesa when the horseman came into sight. He rode in swiftly from the north, heels out from the animal's flanks, elbows jutting from his sides.

'Balthazar.' Sanchez was first to identify the big brown hat and flapping chaps. 'Why does the fool use the horse so in this heat?'

'Could be there is something amiss,' another suggested.

Balthazar splashed his way across the creek.

'Miguel!' he shouted. 'You must come to the house. Pronto!' The ramrod walked towards the man. Vallery stood watching from the shade.

'What?' Sanchez rapped.

'Montoya,' the man panted. 'He is to be whipped.'

Sanchez's face tightened. 'Whipped? For what reason?'

'He was caught stealing at the house. The patron, he is very angry. I fear for Montoya . . . When I saw the dust from out here I think it is you and I come.' Balthazar's gaze swept the others. 'You must all come.'

Vallery saw Sanchez's face pale as he dropped his stogie and ground it out beneath his heel. Then Oteros strode across to confront the foreman.

'This must not happen, Miguel,' he said darkly. 'Montoya is not a strong *hombre*. He shall not be whipped.'

Dev noted the man said 'shall not', not 'should not'.

'Be silent!'

Sanchez turned and stared directly at Vallery. There might have been a hint of warning in the man's hard stare; he could not be sure.

Then the tall man was swinging astride as the messenger said, 'We must hurry, *amigo* Miguel.'

'Perhaps it is time!'

The foreman's words sounded somehow ominous to their ears. Then Sanchez shouted, 'Holla!' and used his spurs. As the horse carried him past Vallery, he called, 'You should wait here, I think it may be best.'

The mob was splashing across the stream as Dev lifted a hand to take the cigarette from between his lips. He was aware he wanted to remain out here, fork his prad and go crawling over the mesa looking for the bull. He knew he had developed quite a skill in avoiding any situation that might put him in direct conflict with Braden, even though there had been times when he felt an itch to horn in, for Braden was a man who always played it hard.

He almost did what he really wanted to do – go climbing up the mesa as the riders' dust faded and blew away. Time passed but his thoughts wouldn't let him be. Then abruptly he reined in as he recalled something specific.

His frown cut hard. Sanchez had said: *Perhaps it is time.* Had that merely been something said in anger, or was it something much more?

He brushed hands down his sweat-stained shirt and sat his saddle motionless for a full five minutes before kicking the mount downslope.

It was five miles to the house.

The first slash of the blacksnake across the man's naked back cracked across the hushed yard like a shot.

'Rand, no! Stop that!'

Braden paused with a flicker of surprise at the sound of his wife's cry from the gallery. His eyes glittered. Then Yancey appeared at her side and placed a restraining hand on her arm as she made to come down the steps. With a grunt, the rancher turned and focused his attention on the man tied to the tack-room upright.

There was a livid mark across the full width of the little man's back. It was not showing blood yet, but it would.

The lash fell again and Montoya's knees buckled. The tie ropes bit into his wrists as he sagged.

'*Madre de Dios*!' gasped handyman Pas Gregorio. 'He is too small an *hombre* for such punishment.'

The yard hands standing within earshot did not speak. They were every bit as shocked as Gregorio but fear of Braden held them silent. They'd seen him in these rages before. It seemed whenever he punished someone it was intended as a warning for all.

The third stroke cracked down.

'Steal from a man who keeps you and your brood alive, would you?' Braden panted. 'By glory, you won't do it again, I promise you.'

Four.

On the gallery an ashen Evalina leaned against the giant and watched with bitter unblinking eyes.

Yancey's face was impassive. The man had a violent past. He had seen it all. A short distance away, Mrs Latimer watched unblinkingly, relishing every stroke.

Five. The women and children from the village watched from the yard fence, and some of the latter were crying. The rest of the house staff, yard hands and the visiting cattle-dealer stood staring, not looking away until distracted by a sudden drum of hoof-beats.

As heads turned, Montoya slumped unconscious.

'Throw a bucket of water over him,' panted Braden. 'His lesson's not through yet.'

'I say it is, *señor!*'

Every head turned to see Miguel Sanchez stepping down from his lathered horse.

CHAPTER 9

BLOOD AND HATE

Braden's eyes snapped wide as he watched the tall lithely moving figure coming towards him. Dust was gusting high out along the south-west trail and it was easy enough to identify the others coming in – Gallardo, Rilla, Balthazar and Benito, still with his arm in a sling from Braden's pick-axe. If the rancher had to list the five of his crew he mistrusted most it would be his ramrod and those four malcontents.

'Just what the blue hell do you think you're about, mister?' He thrust the whip to arm's length in Sanchez's direction. 'You halt right there, pilgrim. That's an order!'

Sanchez kept coming. This was all wrong, he knew. It was premature and might ruin all his plans. But he'd reached the point of no return. He'd been scheming and nursing his hatreds so long they'd suddenly burst their banks. His friends were behind him, he knew he could rely on others if he first

showed the way. No more waiting for help or messi-
ahs that would likely never show anyway. This was the
hour.

His eyes flaring defiantly now, Braden shook out
the whip, hauled it over his shoulder and lay another
tremendous cut across Montoya's skinny shoulders.
There was a gasp of shock from servants and yard
hands, and all eyes cut to the ramrod who seemed to
hesitate, then came on.

Braden couldn't believe it. The whip fell to
ground and he reefed at the handle of the .44-.40 at
his hip.

'No, Rand!'

Evalina was on the main gallery with the silhouette
of the housekeeper in back of her.

'Get back inside, woman—' Braden began, then
broke off sharply, realizing that danger was drawing
too close. He cocked the gun deliberately and aimed
at Sanchez's chest.

'One more step and it will be your last – greaser!'

Sanchez propped and the crowd seemed to hold
its breath. He turned his head. His sidekicks had
reached the gate and were stepping down, grim-
faced and reassuring. He hooked a thumb in his
holster as he turned back to Braden.

'You go too far, *señor*. Too far with Montoya, too far
with all of us—'

'I'm ready to pull this trigger, mister. You know me
too well to think I'd back down to the likes of you.'
The weapon flicked to cover the four approaching
warily across the yard. 'Another step and you're all
fired. Two more steps and you'll be fired upon. Men,

127

support your master!'

Suddenly every man – those in the watching semi-circle and those at the house – seemed stricken deaf; it was like the cattleman's eye was poison – nobody wanted to catch it.

'You see,' Sanchez said with rising excitement. He made a sweeping gesture. 'Nobody will help you, rich man. Why, because every soul here today has been touched by your greed and cruelty and—'

The Colt in Braden's hand exploded with a deafening bellow. Everybody jumped. They expected to see Sanchez fall. But the shot was deliberately aimed high – a warning.

Gallardo didn't know that.

Positioned on Braden's flank, the pock-marked *vaquero* got his gun out and jerked trigger. He fired too fast. Instead of striking its target the slug struck ground ten feet in front of Braden but then ricocheted upwards, blinding the man with dust and grit.

Sanchez dived. Seizing Braden's gun arm he banged it down on his upraised thigh, jerking the weapon loose. The rancher roared and retaliated with a swing that had all his weight behind it. Sanchez took the mean hit flush on the jaw and was sent reeling. Braden made a lunge for his weapon but slid to a halt when he realized a big foot was standing on it.

Rilla gave a gap-toothed grin. It was meant to show how relaxed he was but his face gave him away. The man was ashen and terrified. Talking about overthrowing the mighty Braden and actually doing something about it were vastly different things, and

128

Rilla was praying Sanchez would do something, anything, to get them out of it.

Braden's face was white as he turned slowly to confront Sanchez. He might well be disarmed and surrounded by hostile men but he showed no trace of fear, just arrogant, affronted rage.

'You treacherous, back-stabbing Judas – after all I've done for you and your miserable mendicant tribe—'

The diatribe cut off as he lunged with the speed of a mountain panther. Sanchez didn't expect it. Next thing he was going over and Braden had one iron hand wrapped round his throat while the other hammered his face. Going down, the man clawed for his shooter, but Braden anticipated. He pistoned a knee into the groin, and as the Mexican doubled up, snatched the pistol free then sprang back with a shout of triumph.

'Next one's in the guts, Rilla!' he warned, punching a shot over the *vaquero*'s big hat. 'That's right, let go of it!' He twisted his head towards the gallery, saw what he was looking for. 'Yancey! Get out here and help me round up this cavvy of mavericks! Move, you great ox!'

'No!'

Evalina's cry came sudden and sharp as the giant at her side stirred. She seized him by the arm. 'No, Rand, it's too dangerous. He doesn't understand . . . don't!'

'Get here!' Braden commanded. 'Remember your oath, you bastard?'

Yancey remembered. There was only so much his

dim mind could absorb, yet he remembered the day
Carrado himself had committed him to accompanying Braden and transferring his full protection to
Evalina, whom he now worshipped. The oath of a
simple man, but not one to be ignored.

Evalina clung to Yancey until he quit the steps,
then fell back, weeping.

'All your fault!' Mrs Latimer sniffed, but the
woman's voice was drowned out by Braden's.

'All right, big fella, collect their hoglegs . . . and
then collect the trash!'

'Trash?' Yancey queried as he closed on Rilla.

'This trash!'

Braden had worked his way close to Sanchez.
Suddenly he pivoted, swinging his revolver like a club
to smash the side of the man's head with brutal force.
The ramrod dropped like a stone and an outraged
Balthazar started forward, managing to avoid a huge
reaching hand.

It was as ugly a sight as Buffalo Gate headquarters
had seen since it changed its name from Rancho
Antiguo, this bloody scene which greeted the lone
rider's eyes when he came careening in off the rangeland and hammered through the open gateway of
the houseyard.

For one hellish moment, Vallery feared he'd shown
up too late.

Then he realized that the familiar figure of
Sanchez was stirring in the dust of the yard, that the
bloody-backed figure hanging unconscious from the
lamp-pole beyond was obviously still breathing.

Even so it was still a tableau filled with uncertainty and his hand hung close to gunbutt as he walked his prad through the congealing silence; Yancey blinking slowly in the harsh light as he stood by four *vaqueros* holding their sixshooters; the ramrod struggling to sit up with blood from his head soaking his shirt; Evalina staring helplessly from the house. Braden watched him with a huge smirk of triumph.

'Here he is. The rainbow cowboy. Always shows up after the storm!'

Dev's expression didn't change as he reined in and glanced across at Montoya. Without a word he pushed the lathered mount across to the lamp-pole, slipped his work-knife from its sheath and severed the wrist ropes with one slash. Montoya fell to the ground.

'See to him,' he ordered the housemaids grouped in the shade, then slid to the ground, letting the reins trail.

There was no telling what he was feeling or thinking as he returned to Braden with every uneasy eye fixed on his tall figure In the time he'd worked for Braden, the Buffalo Gate's one-name mystery man had earned a lot of respect, particularly for a gringo. He'd even made several half-friends in Sanchez, Benito and Mrs Braden and one or two others, even if he mightn't appear especially friendly at that moment.

Nor did Braden.

'I give the orders, mister.'

Dev halted, hands on hips.

'That's mostly the case.' He turned to the women

who were approaching Montoya hesitantly. He gestured. 'Move along, that man needs attention.'

Braden wasn't looking cocky any longer.

'Be very careful, loser. Your interfering with my authority won't get you any—'

'You were wrong and you know it.' Dev's voice was quiet but carried weight. 'Now let's see about getting this closed down before it flares up again.'

'Judas Priest . . .' Braden began, then realized the ramrod was on his feet. His eyes snapped cold. 'Well, what are you waiting for, you double-dealing sidewinder? Why aren't you riding?'

Sanchez was still groggy from the head blow. He was having trouble focusing, much less understanding.

'What?' he said uncertainly.

'Hear that?' Braden was diverted when he saw his wife and the housekeeper approaching. Around the yard, people were still waiting and staring, uncertain whether they'd witnessed it all or not. 'Dismiss!' he shouted, gesticulating. 'But not you bums!' he added, stabbing a finger at Sanchez's disarmed *vaqueros*. 'You'll move when I say . . . do what I say.' He turned back to stare hard at Dev. 'Like everybody on my land does. Right, mister?' Vallery shrugged and the man turned to Sanchez. 'Still here?'

'*Sí.*'

'Better not be in five minutes. If you are, you'll be hog-tied, loaded in a wagon and hauled into Fort James to the sheriff's office where you'll be charged with attempted murder.'

'Please, Rand,' Evalina said, 'don't be too harsh. It

was all an unfortunate mix-up, I'm sure Miguel didn't mean to harm you.'

Twin spots of anger showed high on Braden's cheekbones.

'Thank you so much, madam, loyal and informed as always!' He swung his broad back on the woman and stabbed a finger at Sanchez. 'You are fired, mister. If you want to be both fired and locked up, I can arrange that.'

Sanchez paled.

'You fire me? I was born on this land. My father owned Rancho Antiguo, would still own it if you had not stolen it from him. You cannot fire me!'

'It's done. Vamoose!'

For some reason Sanchez looked appealingly at Vallery, who just shrugged. He felt powerless to interfere; he was in no way certain he still had a job on the Gate himself.

Sanchez cursed and gazed around, chest heaving with emotion. Everywhere he looked he encountered downcast eyes, averted faces. And when he looked at Braden he saw nothing for a moment but the red film of hate clouding his eyes. His hand darted inside his leather vest. His fingers closed over the butt of a two-shot derringer. It came whipping out but was never fired as iron fingers closed over his wrist, jerked and the tiny pistol fell to the ground.

'Don't be loco, man,' panted Dev, maintaining his grip.

Sanchez threw a blow, but was restricted and off-balance. Dev held on to his man until the mad look left his face, then thrust him away.

'Hmm, might have just saved yourself a similar fate, Dev,' Braden said with some satisfaction. 'All right, Sanchez, get moving and be off my land with your belongings by sundown.' He signalled to the disarmed men grouped uneasily in the background. 'The same applies to you. You're all through and if you're not gone by dark I'll have my ramrod run you off.'

'What ramrod?' challenged a defiant Benito. 'You just fired him.'

'This ramrod,' Braden retorted, clapping a hand to Vallery's shoulder. He grinned broadly. 'Surprised? You shouldn't be.'

'I don't figure . . .' Dev frowned. 'One minute you were warning me, now. . . ?'

'I pay my debts.' Braden paused to jam a cigar between his teeth and light up. He puffed luxuriously as he watched the four *vaqueros* slouching away. He stared at a white-faced Sanchez and jerked his jaw at him, signalling him to follow the others.

'Better go, Miguel,' Vallery advised.

Sanchez made no response until a jittery yard hand led his horse across to him. It was only after he'd fitted boot to stirrup and swung up that his gaze seemed to clear, then began to blaze.

'I shall go,' he said with dignity. 'I shall go because alone I can not stand against you and your great evil, *señor*. But I shall return to this earth that should be mine. One day I shall come back and you shall die as you are a man of great evil. If you never believed anything before in your foul life, you can believe this.'

His gaze came to rest on Vallery and his voice dropped, but still held great bitterness.

'You too, Dev. I believed you were a man, a true *hombre*. But I find you are just a willing slave, like all the others. It is an evil thing you have done here today and shall cost you dear. Today we might have triumphed but you turned the scales. So, sleep with one eye open also, gringo, for one night I will be there.'

'Well, what are you waiting for?' Braden barked at Dev as the tall man turned his horse and rode away. 'He threatened your life. Are you going to take that?'

'Shut up, Braden.'

Braden paled. 'You dare say that to me?'

'That and more. You've overplayed your hand this time. You're lucky all this didn't cost you your life.'

He turned away to see hands toting a by now conscious Montoya to the house, and was about to call after them when Braden moved to block his line of vision.

'Give me one good reason why I shouldn't fire you as well – then fire off a wire to a certain marshal?'

Vallery stared at the man stonily. He was in a dark mood now. He'd done what he'd felt he must, yet felt anything but good about it.

'Can't think of one,' he grunted impassively.

'All right, relax, relax,' Braden said, that big-toothed smile back in place. 'I was only joshing. You still want that job or don't you?'

Vallery wanted to tell him to go straight to hell. It should have been easy enough to do. Yet gazing round at the worried faces, and conscious of

Evalina's pleading gaze, he realized he couldn't just walk, tempting though it might be.

'Why me, Braden?' he asked dully.

'Aren't you forgetting something, mister?' The big man sounded genuinely grateful, friendly almost. 'You warned me there was something in the wind days ago, and by God and by glory you were dead on target. I might be a hard man but I pay my debts. And I owe you big – ramrod Dev.'

At evening a little wind murmured amongst the trees bordering the stream. The shadows climbed up the steep slopes, reaching for the summits. On the sandy banks, rabbits sat quiet and still.

Suddenly, from the direction of the foothills came the sound of hoofbeats muffled by the dry summer grass. The rabbits sped noiselessly for cover. A white crane rose from the stream and flapped away with slow, heavy wingbeats. For a long moment the whole scene was lifeless, then the lone rider emerged from the trees and came into the open along the sandy bank.

Miguel Sanchez had undergone a dramatic change in appearance in just a few days since his flight from Buffalo Gate.

Seemingly crushed by defeat, bitterness and fading hopes the tall *vaquero*, with his black hair unkempt and mustache looking ragged, he now wore the gaunt, unshaven look of a man who'd lost something vital, something that might never be reclaimed.

Prior to his dismissal, Sanchez had truly believed he had many friends and supporters both on and off the ranch who both knew of the injustice done him and were ready and even eager to support his fight for 'his' land when and if the time came.

Reality had proven far different.

Suddenly in many quarters where he'd once been welcomed, he was now a tainted man. He was no longer the respected straw boss of the biggest ranch in the region, but had become Braden's enemy, and Braden had called in all his loyalty markers both in the region and in Fort James.

True, his former ranch henchmen were still sticking, and some were due to meet him here tonight. But they weren't the same brave *amigos* of before. Out of work, ostracized by many for the same reason as himself, Gallardo, Rilla, Balthazar and Benito still bragged about the 'revolution' to come, and cursed Braden and Dev and the whole cowardly crew who should have all quit when they were dismissed.

But they were not convincing, and, of course, underlying their changed attitude was the unspoken thing that stood between him and them now. Carrado.

Even Miguel no longer had any hopes of Carrado.

Maybe he had been a fool ever to have believed the rumors and whispers that the *paisano* rebel fighter had escaped prison and was rumored to be making his way north to seek vengeance against a 'big *ranchero*' over something to do with a woman. Knowing what he knew, half-knew and speculated upon regarding Braden's journey into Mexico several years ago on business, from which he'd returned with a beautiful young bride amid a blaze of

137

gossip and conjecture, Sanchez had set out to uncover as much as possible about that bizarre affair.

He was eventually convinced that Evalina Braden was the one and the same Evalina Aragon who had reputedly ridden the danger trails of Mexico with Carrado in some of his more famous battles on behalf of the 'shirtless ones' of Chihuahua and Sonora.

He believed that if that story were true, a free Carrado must surely show up in the county sooner or later to reclaim his woman and, hopefully, avenge himself against the man who'd enslaved her.

It was weeks now since the first whisper of Carrado's escape from prison and his flight north had electrified the plotters, but since then, nothing. He'd had hope then. Now he just drank and drifted and sat hatching schemes he knew he could never pull off. Just another Mex loser in a region overrun with that breed already.

He pulled his sixshooter at the sound of a horse, put it away as Rilla and Balthazar came out of the trees and rode across the sand.

The trio made a fire and were lacing their coffee with tequila when Gallardo arrived with a long face and a three-day growth. He'd tried for a job on Bona Vista that day and had been rejected because nobody would hire any of the former Buffalo Gate hands.

The four sat on logs trying to cheer one another up when hoofbeats sounded. They were free men on open land, yet all cleared their pistols as they waited for the riders to show. They were expecting Benito but there was no doubting that they could hear two or more horses coming through the brush.

It turned out to be just two, stocky Benito wearing a huge smile which they didn't understand at first, and, riding behind him, a lean stranger wearing a yellow sombrero.

'*Buenos noches, compañeros!*' called the ex-cook. 'I bring along a poor *peon* I meet along the trail.'

They glared uncomprehendingly, and it wasn't until the horsemen rode into the firelight that they realized he seemed vaguely familiar. His hair was shoulder-length, his handsome face had a wild wolf look, and he greeted them as if he knew them.

'*Hola!*' he shouted, reining in and fingering back his big floppy hat. Then, 'You, *amigo*,' he said, indicating Sanchez. 'You would be the one the fat one brings me to see, no?'

That was when the bell ran.

'Madonna!' Sanchez breathed. 'Could it be. . . ?'

'Could be and is,' Benito said proudly. 'He was searching for us brave rebels, and he found me. So, where are the manners, *caballeros?* Say *buenos noches* and welcome to the noble Carrado.'

'How does that feel, José?'

Vallinova the wrangler rose from the bench in the bunkhouse and gingerly placed his weight on his right leg. He frowned, then grinned in delight.

'She is better, Dev. How do you know so much about the bumps and bruises?'

'I guess I fall off horses a lot,' Vallery said easily, tossing aside the bandage roll he'd used to tape the injured man's leg. The rider had been thrown from his mount when about to accompany Evalina Braden on a visit to the Mexican village. The hand smiled bravely as he tried the leg out again, then nodded.

'I can still go with the *señora, gracias* to you.'

'Forget it,' Dev grunted, getting his hat. 'I'll handle that chore for you. You need to rest up.'

He stretched his arms and stifled a yawn. He didn't sleep much any more. The new job was demanding and he added many hours to it, riding solitary night patrols. There'd been no trouble on Buffalo Gate since the Sanchez incident, yet he still was not reassured. Braden was convinced that having been bested so convincingly and then fired, Sanchez and his henchmen would talk a lot and make threats – and that was about all they could do before fading into the background amongst the Mexican unemployed of Fort James.

Dev was not so sure.

Evalina was delighted when he announced his intention of accompanying her to the village. It was her regular habit to visit the Mexican women and help out those who might be ill or in need.

Her husband tolerated this 'peculiarity' of hers and didn't stand in her way, providing she was always escorted. He insisted that concern for her security was his reason, but when in frivolous mood she joked that Braden was afraid she might take advantage of these visits to run off with some good-looking cowpuncher or another.

Today, of course, they were also accompanied on the two-mile journey across the slopes by Yancey, who toted the food and medical supplies that accompanied her on these visits.

Vallery strolled around the village talking with the women and children while Evalina was busy, but joined her when she visited the Montoya shack.

The *vaquero* was recovering fast from his whipping. These people were tough because they had to be. Evalina was serious while she dressed the man's back and issued instructions to his wife, but as soon as they quit the house she was laughing and joking again, teasing Vallery because she thought he looked so serious.

She was right about that. He was serious, and her light mood this week wasn't helping him feel any less that way, for reasons he intended keeping to himself for the time being.

'I don't understand your long face, Dev, I truly don't. Or perhaps the responsibility of your new job is beginning to tell? Is that it?'

'My long face . . . your sparkle,' he replied. 'There's a contrast for you.' He studied her closely. 'How come, lady? We have a big ruckus where some people are hurt and others are sacked, yet almost ever since you seem to act like life has taken a turn for the better. You want to explain that one to me?'

They'd reached the stage where they could be reasonably open with one another. He'd always suspected she hated Braden's guts although she never confirmed or denied that impression. At unguarded moments he might see her staring at the big man with eyes like drills. He knew Braden beat his wife and that galled him, but there was a limit to what he could do about that.

141

If she was some kind of prisoner here, the same went for him, double. Every time he looked over the ranch's boundaries he reminded himself that the fences were little different from Yuma's high walls. Sure, he could quit any time he wanted. But sometimes that ancient mariner's warning of the unknown land beyond the sea rim came to mind: *Beyond this place there be dragons.*

For her, he brooded, the dragons – or dragon – was right here. Braden was in control.

She looked at the sky and swung her basket.

'Oh, it's just that everything seems to be going so well now the round-up's over and things are settling down to normal, I guess.' She gave him a sideways glance, serious now. 'Now it's your turn. Why so serious?'

He simply shrugged.

He had no intention of bothering her with his concerns, yet he felt tempted to bring up the matter of the persistent whispers concerning a certain Mexican troublemaker with whom she was said to have been once connected.

He'd encountered an old hunter at the south gate three days earlier. During their conversation the gabby oldster had idly remarked:

'Hey, pardner, what do you hear about that no-account hellraiser from Mexico they say's been sighted this side of the river? You know, Caracas or Carrado – whatever they call him? Folks here are getting nervous on account wherever he shows up anyplace all the Mexes start getting excited and worked up and start wanting to kick us out. You worried about that?'

He'd just shaken his head and continued on his way. But ever since then he'd doubled his patrols of the ranch borders, had questioned the hands without learning anything more on the Carrado rumor; tried to keep tabs on Sanchez without much success.

He wanted to believe the whispers were just harmless fantasy and gossip, but would have found that easier to digest were it not for the change in the woman at his side today.

And the 'ifs' kept coming. What if the stories about Evalina and Carrado were all true? 'If' she really had been traded to Braden following the rebel's capture in Mexico, as rumored, and 'if' the rumors that Carrado had busted jail and shot his way north had substance?

The next place they visited on their rounds was timely. There the woman of the house insisted he drink some wine, as he looked so weary. Vallery had one excellent glass, then another. By the time they were heading back for headquarters he was feeling relaxed for the first time in days.

Relaxed enough to raise at least the very question which he'd convinced himself earlier he should steer away from. Namely, had she heard the rumors of Carrado's crossing the border?

'Oh, of course.' She didn't seem fazed. Then she laughed. 'I honestly thought people had forgotten that idiotic story surrounding my marriage in Chihuahua, but I suppose it's too outlandish a fable to just let die.'

Then she glanced up at him sharply.

'You surely don't believe it, Dev?'

'Why should I?' he parried, eyes on the trail. Then he shrugged. 'In any case, even if it was true, what could I do about it? Or anybody?'

He waited for a reply. It was slow in coming.

'True, true. There's only one person I know who could ever do anything about such a situation – if it was true. Just one . . .'

That was all that was said.

He actually rested an hour in the ramrod's quarters that afternoon, ate a hearty supper and almost convinced himself he was relaxing.

Yet midnight found him far from the hacienda, checking on the nighthawks and patrolling the boundaries once again.

Nothing.

It was almost morning before he turned in. He slept until six then was up in the saddle again.

Beyond the line-rider's shack in the canyon on the old Darcy place, the night was dark and quiet. Inside it was very different as a dozen dark-faced men wearing charro pants and big hats sat listening intently to the only genuinely relaxed-looking man present.

'Rumours, legends, lies and fairy tales,' drawled Carrado, spurred boots crossed on the old table, an unlit stogie between his teeth. He snapped his fingers. 'They spin them all around me and all are false. I am but a simple man of flesh and weakness who wants nothing but to be with men of courage and ideals when they meet together to plot out their sacred destiny. Who has the match?'

They traded eager looks. The group, which was growing larger by the day, could not help but admire the way the rascal-hero from over the border was able to put simple notions into the kind of words that helped a man dispel uncertainty and geared up his courage.

And each man present from Miguel Sanchez down to the youthful abattoir hand from Fort James enjoying his first 'freedom assembly' tonight was aware that what was being proposed would surely require courage.

Carrado himself had emphasized early that – should they vote to attack the Buffalo Gate – even courage, high ideals and quick guns might not be enough. 'If . . .' Carrado paused to blow a smoke-ring at the ceiling. 'If the hour has indeed come and the worm shall turn, then let there be no mistake how success may be won.' He held up a finger. 'By force.'

He suddenly dropped his boots to the floor and stood tall, a swaggering figure with black eyes which drilled and held.

'That Braden seized the ranch from the father of Miguel with the help of corrupt officials, by bribing officers in the Land and Titles Bureau, there is little doubt. But before and during the great theft of your birthright that *hombre* recruited force, bought force and used force more recklessly than a crooked *alcalde* passing out election promises. In the end he wore down old Sanchez and claimed his prize. So I say that that which is stolen by force can only be reclaimed by force.' A pause. 'Is there any *caballero* here who disagrees?'

145

Silence.

Some of the dispossessed poor present had been living on dreams for years. Others, such as the ex-Gate riders, were consumed by hate and resentment. Only a very few, such as Sanchez, were fired by a genuine idealistic need to right a great wrong.

And it was probable that there was but one *vaquero* present, who, although just as inspired as any other, found he could not separate the excitement of the great plan from the human cost it might entail.

Two hours later, with the final plans in place and great oaths taken before the first bottle of tequila was produced, this odd man out lighted a cheroot, adjusted the sling on his arm and slipped away, hoping nobody would notice he had gone.

Yet someone did.

Vallery was just beginning to doze when he heard it. It was a cry which sounded as though the person was fighting against crying out, and it barely penetrated the stillness of his darkened room.

He rose on one elbow, reluctant to come fully awake and maybe say goodbye to that welcome drowsy feeling he'd been courting all night.

He was beginning to nod again when he heard a thud, a muffled voice, then, as he sat up, the voices from just outside by the cookshack.

Going to the window he saw first the silhouettes of the two night patrollers, then noticed lights on at the house.

The nightwatch sounded concerned, he thought; he still didn't want to take it any further, yet knew he must.

146

A minute later he emerged fully dressed just as the pair were about to move off on their rounds.

'What's going on?' he demanded gruffly.

'Ahh, it is the *ranchero* we think, Señor Dev,' replied the senior man. 'We think maybe . . .' He tilted his hand to make the universal sign for drinking.

'I'll take care of it,' he growled and the pair hurried off towards the barn. No *vaquero* in his right mind wanted to mess with Braden, sober or drunk.

He didn't need this, Vallery brooded as he stared across the yard. But the fact that one of the lights showing came from Evalina Braden's quarters was in no way reassuring.

Then he heard her cry out, followed by Braden's deep voice, thick with anger and whiskey.

Even now he hesitated. His relationship with his employer was an edgy one. Braden valued his abilities, he knew, but that was about as far as it went. In return, Dev regarded his employer as scum – rich, successful and powerful without doubt – but scum nonetheless.

The huge factor remained that Braden had provided a safe house for him such as he'd never had since he'd been on the run. He was loath to risk another clash that might threaten his security here. But when he heard the crash of breaking glass and saw a curtain flick, he knew he had no choice.

He crossed quickly to the western gallery and was striding along it when he found his way suddenly blocked by a familiar figure.

147

'No!' Yancey's voice held authority. 'No business. Dev goes away.'

He backed up a step. 'The hell you say. Get out of my way or I'll—'

'You only make worse. Soon he will fall asleep from whiskey.'

'What if he kills her first, damn you?'

'Yancey will stop.'

'Why aren't you stopping it now, you great humbug? What sort of a protector are you, anyway?'

'Yancey must not be sent away. Must stay on ranch to watch over missy.'

There were no sounds to be heard from further along at the moment. Although far from reassured, Vallery was curious enough to put a query that had nagged him for some time.

'Nobody's that loyal. You're either too scared to do what you should, or you don't really give a damn about that lady.'

He saw that hit home hard. The giant frame seemed to shake.

'Not right. Yancey take oath to protect, so he protect.'

'An oath? An oath to whom?'

'No say. Secret.'

Vallery's mind worried at the information he was getting like a dog at a bone. He was sifting through what he knew, or thought he knew, about what had happened at the Palo Pinto Ranch of Emil Conrade below the border three years ago, about who had been involved and who it was said had been.

He took a shot in the dark.

'Carrado?'

He saw his shaft go home. The great head nodded.

'You not tell—'

'Yeah, yeah, I know – big secret.' Dev was staring ahead now, worrying about the silence. He had to know what was happening, if anything. He put a hand on a massive arm.

'I'm just going to take a look, big fella.' He held up his palms. 'No trouble. Promise.'

He stepped nimbly by, walked quickly to the first door and entered the hacienda's west wing. He found Evalina's room in darkness and silence. Reassured some, but not enough, he took the by now familiar route leading to the library, main dining-room and Braden's study.

The door to the study stood open with light spilling out. As he approached silently he heard voices. He halted.

'Perhaps those losers who work for me are right . . . what they say behind my back . . . Do you think they're right, Mrs Latimer? You know, when they say I'm cracking up and drinking too much . . . turning on my wife . . .'

'Of course not, Mr Braden. What would such people know about anything? You are simply under a great deal of strain, is all. It is all the trouble with Sanchez . . . the rumors . . .'

'What rumors? Continue, pray, woman. To what rumors do you refer?'

'S-sir I only mean what the servants are saying about that infamous Carrado . . . you know how they talk . . .'

149

'Yes, and how you take notice. Get out.'

'But, Mr Braden—'

'Out!'

Vallery stepped into a recessed doorway as the housekeeper emerged and hurried by, her profile pale and drawn. When she was gone he emerged to stare at the doorway, fighting a battle with himself. What to do? Confront the man and risk everything by taking him to task? Or play yellow dog and simply disappear, then wait until he attacked Evalina the next time? And there would be a next time. He strode for the doorway and entered. Braden was slumped asleep across his desk with an empty bottle in one hand. He could awake him and maybe risk getting fired, when he would be unable to help Evalina or anyone else. Or he could defer the show-down until another time and maybe trust to luck.

It was hard to turn and walk away, but he did it.

CHAPTER 10

BATTLE AT BUFFALO GATE

The day destined to be unlike any other dawned soft and clear, its timid grey light picking out the figure of the tall rider with the golden beard already miles out from the hacienda at this early hour as he approached the south-eastern boundary fence.

It had become his custom to ride almost constant patrol on the fences until he could rid himself of the by now ingrained feeling that the mood, tempo and rhythm of Buffalo Gate were somehow askew.

He'd have done no less on his own little spread at Flint River under similar circumstances; he was obliged to do it here.

He rode several miles before sighting the horse. It was riderless with reins hanging loose as it came mooching out of a stand of aspen, cropping at the dew damp grass.

His first thought was for his nightriders, and, gun drawn, he spurred swiftly across the grassy depression to enter the trees, where he sighted the figure by the log almost immediately. He kicked his way across as the man slowly raised his bloody head, and realized it was Benito the cook, the man who'd tried to kill him and afterwards had become a kind of a friend.

'*Amigo*,' was the man's first words. Then: 'Water!'

He drank, and the story came out in short painful sentences. About Carrado the gringo-fighter, the plot with Sanchez to overthrow Braden, take him down and rescue Carrado's woman, the rancher's wife.

He began to relate how he'd slipped away from last night's meeting to try and warn his '*amigo* Dev', only to be detected by Sanchez and brutally beaten as a traitor. It was only when he recovered consciousness in the early hours that he'd somehow managed to get mounted to make it as far as the boundary before collapsing.

By this time Vallery was back in his saddle tossing down his canteen and grub sack. No time for anything. He raked horsehide with spur, careening across the cattle pastures for headquarters at a racing gallop, praying he would not be too late.

But he still had long miles to cover when above the drumming hoofbeats he heard the savage sound of gunfire.

With smoke stinging his eyes, Braden stared stupidly at the dead man who'd seemingly plummeted from the sky to crash to the steps almost at his feet. Then he realized it was Lino Perea whom he'd positioned on the roof soon after the shooting began.

How many losses did that make? Far more important, how many were left?

In the mere moments the master of Buffalo Gate had had to absorb the shock of the attack, he'd realized two vital realities. Firstly, the enemy with Carrado and Sanchez leading them in were few enough. But the brutal shocks were that, one: his outriders had plainly made no attempt to halt the invasion, and two: no more than a mere handful of his hacienda force was making any pretence of defence.

A roar of pure rage shook his powerful body, only to be drowned out by something louder, more penetrating.

'Liberty and justice!' came the battle cry from somewhere across the besieged yard. The rancher punched three shots in that direction, then ducked low as answering bullets whistled through the smoke fog.

Braden was seeing it, living it, yet still could not believe it.

No one on the Buffalo Gate could.

The headquarters had been just beginning to stir when uncomprehending eyes looked out to see the yard seemingly filled with grim-faced men with rifles and pistols – familiar faces, mostly, but seemingly led by a wild-looking stranger, who was the one demanding Braden come out and surrender to the 'freedom fighters' of Buffalo Gate.

Still half-asleep but apprehensive, Braden had

come lunging from his front door with a gun, someone had touched off the first shot and now, a half-
hour later, chaos reigned.

Men were dying and the hay barn was ablaze as the
cattle king bawled orders that sent a mere handful of
hands to stem the new onrush of horsemen now
attacking the east wing.

As the men disappeared, Braden darted to a
broken window to trigger three times at the crouch-
ing, racing figure of former hand Gallardo as he
galloped his mangy horse across Mrs Latimer's petu-
nia beds, shooting like a fool.

Abruptly Gallardo threw up his arms and crashed
from the saddle, the wild-eyed animal swerving away
from the hacienda to vanish beyond the corrals.

Dev Vallery saw Gallardo fall.

It was his first glimpse of the actual violence and
even though anticipating the worst, he could scarcely
believe that any situation could deteriorate so swiftly.
He brought his horse cutting around the corrals,
shouting for a cease-fire at the top of his lungs.
Whether anybody could hear he had no way of knowing. A rifle roared from close by through the smoke
haze. His mount missed its footing, then dropped its
head and crashed down abruptly, hurling him high
to strike ground with brutal force.

Dazed, spitting dirt and fumbling for his sixgun, in
that instant Vallery became just another part of a
madness in which few men seemed clear on what was
happening, and why.

The tall man in the outsized hat lunging into
Braden's sacred study may well have been the only

one who understood it all. Fighting for causes was all too familiar to Carrado, and there was never a cause that meant more to the rebel fighter. Outwardly nonchalant, inwardly in turmoil, Carrado was in frantic search of his woman, and went rushing from room to room while bullets tore through timber and brick and the jagged scream of a mortally hit man filled the passageway like something from a nightmare.

Reaching the end of the hallway he almost crashed into a wild-eyed kitchen hand toting a big knife. His blow merely felled the blubbering man to his knees; he hauled him dazedly to his feet again.

'Evalina!' he panted. 'Where is my woman?'

Before the man could reply, ghostly figures appeared through the invading smoke. One was a white-faced Braden. Instantly Carrado released his victim and triggered fast. Too fast. Braden took cover in a recess and in the instant the gringo-fighter was gone.

Almost insane with blood lust and rage, Braden was tempted for a moment to give chase. Only for a moment. He now realized the fight was being lost and likely nothing could save him but a hostage.

A hostage that would cower them all – Carrado, the traitor Sanchez, double-dealing Vallery – the bastard!

Within dangerous seconds he was at the door that opened on to the gallery, slipping on blood as he steadied himself.

A familiar voice:

'Stay! No, go out.'

Yancey!

'But we'll burn ... I must find Gabriel, please, Yancey, for God's sake—'

Evalina's voice caught in her throat as Braden's shape filled the doorway.

'Good work, Yancey,' he panted, 'She's my ticket out of this—'

'Bad man,' the giant said, and the pistol in his fist drove a lance of white hot agony through Braden's shoulder, hammering him backwards. He triggered back and Yancey began to go down on one side like a house with a collapsing pier. As Braden lunged back towards the door a fusillade of bullets came howling close, and with an animal groan of frustration he spun and disappeared in the shrouding smoke. Moments later Dev Vallery was in the room, stepping over Yancey's body and seizing Evalina by the hand. No time for words. The house was fully ablaze, and though confusion reigned, they somehow made it safely out to the free-standing meathouse. Cautioning a white-faced Evalina to stay put, Vallery leaned from the doorway to squint towards the sound of guns but his vision was suddenly blocked out by the towering shape of the man on horseback.

'Judas!' Miguel Sanchez raged. His shot scorched Vallery's arm and ricocheted madly round the room.

Instantly his gun answered at point-blank range and the dream was over for Miguel Sanchez as he tumbled slowly from his horse and hit ground face down. Two men saw Sanchez fall, one a desperate rancher dashing from one point to another rallying

156

his defenders, the other a big-hatted Mexican ripping open one door door after another in search of his woman. Dev was kneeling at Evalina's side where she'd lost balance dodging the ricochet, when he heard the sudden brutal argument of the sixguns seemingly just outside.

He leapt to the door in time to see Braden walking backwards across the sand with a sudden, third eye in his forehead, before him the tall stranger in the outsized sombrero.

Dev raised his gun to fire but the cry behind him held him.

'No! No, Dev!' Evalina cried, and rushed past him to be swept up in the stranger's arms.

Dev sagged against the doorframe. He stood listening as the clash of conflict began to fade. He realized it was over. The two men who'd fought for the land were dead, and their dying had sapped the morning of its crimson madness.

After a time he stirred himself and walked away slowly to check on the wounded. The weeping man and woman didn't seem to notice he'd gone.

Vallery finished packing his war bag and toted it outside. The fires were out and wounded men were being attended to across the yard on the galleries. The dead? He didn't know many or where they lay at the moment, but someone had taken care of them.

The reality was, that despite the ferocity of the battle which seemingly none but Braden and Sanchez had really wanted, only five had died. The hacienda lay in smoking ruins, someone was weeping softly, but everywhere were people, dazed, shocked yet numbly grateful to be still alive.

Benito, who'd somehow made his own way to headquarters, was seated on a tankstand munching on a tortilla. He used the tortilla as a pointer.

'See, *amigo* Dev – the mesa!' he said.

Vallery stared south. Moving across the slope of the distant mesa were the barely visible shapes of two riders. He didn't need to see them clearly to know who they were. It had taken the gringo-fighter three long years to come after the woman whom an evil man had stolen from him, and she had somehow endured those years simply because she'd always known he would come.

He blinked, and when he looked again they were gone.

His replacement horse was ready for the trail by the time the first people from town came in along the main trail. He would stay only long enough to outline what had taken place, then go. A man like himself couldn't risk becoming involved in inquiries, post mortems, investigations.

He'd often felt a prisoner here yet it always felt safe. He was uneasy now. He feared he might discover that . . . *Beyond this place there be dragons.*

He talked some with a sheriff then went inside to visit the wounded and make his goodbyes. Emerging from a side door, he looked back at Evalina's room, and smiled. He wasn't sure what sort of uncertain future a wild one like Carrado might have in store, but he reckoned if he stuck with her she'd temper his fires.

He'd almost reached his horse before he realized there was a man standing by it. He was grey, he was gaunt, and he wore a badge.

His hand half-started towards his gun, then halted. He couldn't believe it, but suddenly he seemed too weary to fight any longer.

'All right, damn you,' he growled. 'How did you find me?'

'No howdys, Vallery?' Marshal Nells smiled. Then he sobered; that suited him better. 'It's all right, man, you don't have to fret.'

'Not fret about going back to Yuma—'

'Listen to me, just listen. This ain't what you think. You see, I had a notion some time back you could be hereabouts. But it was only a hunch and I had other work to attend to. But I was always still coming, only before I could – it happened, didn't it?'

'What did?' Dev asked wearily, like an old, old man.

'Three weeks ago Marshal Tomkins shot and mortally wounded a thief named Homer. The man was toting a watch with the initials E.C. engraved upon the lid. They cross-questioned him, and realizing he was dying, he confessed to killing Emil Conrade – the man the law claimed you killed at Flint River. He left a signed dying deposition to that effect. Guess we felt bad about what you'd been through, so the Chief Marshal told me to go ahead and come down here to see if I could still find you and give you the news and our apology. Hear what I'm saying, son? Reckon you'll be going home now, huh?'

It seemed an eternity before he could reply.

'Home, Marshal?' he said wonderingly. 'You know, I guess I will at that.'